Sophia Scarlotti
and Ceecee

Books by Anita MacRae Feagles

The Year the Dreams Came Back
Sophia Scarlotti and Ceecee

Anita MacRae
Feagles

Sophia Scarlotti and Ceecee

ATHENEUM · NEW YORK

1979

LIBRARY OF CONGRESS CATALOGING IN PUBLICATION DATA

Feagles, Anita MacRae.
Sophia Scarlotti and Ceecee.

SUMMARY: Ceecee's sixteenth summer is one of many
changes, all of which affect her relationship
with her alter ego, Sophia Scarlotti.
[1. Identity—Fiction]   I. Title.
PZ7.F295So   [Fic]   78-12630
ISBN 0-689-30680-6

Published simultaneously in Canada by
McClelland & Stewart, Ltd.
Manufactured by The Book Press, Brattleboro, Vermont
Designed by Mary M. Ahern
First Printing January 1979
Second Printing September 1979

Sophia Scarlotti
and Ceecee

I

"It is only a few days I have known you," José was saying. "But it seems as if we had always been friends."

Sophia smiled and looked across the table at him. She took another sip of champagne. Her only jewel, a large sapphire, glinted in the soft light of the chandelier that lit the ship's small lounge. She said, "We have spent many hours in each other's company."

"Yes. And in only two days time the ship will dock."

She glanced down. She did not want him to see her chagrin, the sudden sadness that flickered across her face. "It has all been so pleasant," she said.

"Pleasant! Sophia, look at me."

She forced herself to look into his intense black eyes. His dark, handsome face was pained. She felt suddenly aware of herself, the simple black gown that hugged her slim tan body, her blonde hair softly brushing her shoulders. Her lip trembled. She said, "Yes? I am looking at you." She laughed tremulously.

"You know it has been more than pleasant," he whispered. "Much more." He leaned back. "I love to look at you," he said. "You are so much more exciting than merely pretty. You are . . . memorable."

"My fiance," Sophia muttered. "He may soon join us again."

"I think not," José said disdainfully. "His seasickness has quite incapacitated him."

"I do feel sad to have been enjoying this journey while he lay ill."

José suddenly leaned forward. "Sophia, I have not said this before, but I must say it now. The time is getting shorter. You must break off this engagement. You must come to Spain with me."

"Surely it is a temporary thing, this attraction we feel."

He smiled. "So at last you admit you feel something as well."

"It is obvious, I am afraid. But one mustn't take such things too seriously."

"No?" His eyebrows shot up. "And what is it we are to take seriously? Your engagement to this pallid young man?"

"I am obligated," she said, looking down again. She could not bear the intensity of his gaze. He seemed so vital as to be almost frightening.

"You feel obligated only to his family, because you are an honorable woman. But you must honor your own feelings as well. And you would not suffer with me. I can give you anything you want."

She dismissed this with a gesture. "Money means nothing to me."

"I understand that you do feel that way." He sighed. "If only you did not." He smiled sadly. "Give me your hand."

With a shaky little smile, she reached across to him. Very slowly, he lifted her fingers to his lips. She suppressed a shiver.

"Sophia," he said softly. "Let us share another bottle of champagne in my stateroom."

"I must be careful not to get tipsy," she said. She followed him down the corridors to his stateroom. The wine was in a bucket; there were flowers everywhere.

"They are for you," José said, waving to indicate the flowers.

"How confident you were that I would accept your invitation."

"Not at all. Only hopeful." He poured two glasses. "To us . . ."

"Ceecee! Cecily Wood, get up. I know you're awake."

Oh no. It was my little sister, Rebecca. Just at the best part.

"Cee*cee!*" This time Rebecca burst into the room. "Look, you don't have to avoid getting up, because Luz and Mom and I have already done all the work. The apartment is cleaned, and the car is all packed. And all you have to do is wind yourself up and walk to the elevator and go down. Preferably with your luggage. Also wearing clothes."

Then I remembered. Oh, fantastic! Today was the day we were going to the island. We were leaving hot New York and going to the place of all lovely summers and childhood memories and adventures. For a moment, I wondered why I hadn't been asked to do any work, and then I remembered about that, too. They were being nice for a reason. But I didn't want to think about it just then. So I got up, not having any other choice. Rebecca went into one of her little routines.

"You're not really *ugly,* just plain," she said, ready to run. "I mean some people actually *like* skinny little girls with long thin noses and sharp chins and mouse hair and—"

"Bug off, Rebecca," I warned.

"Some people could conceivably be *attracted* to a—" I got her with my pillow. She yelped.

"Get out of here you lumpy little rat," I said, and

she ran off giggling, scampering like a child. She's thirteen most of the time, sometimes acts five, sometimes fifty. She's smart and a horrendous wiseass and adores being outrageous, it's her whole style. I don't mind her, though. Sometimes she goes too heavy and can be irritating, but most of the time I can take her. Not everyone can.

I got out of bed and looked around my room like a stranger. I feel like that every morning because it takes me such a long time to get into being awake. As usual when I looked around my room, I liked it. It was once supposed to be the maid's room in the apartment and looks out over absolutely nothing and is about two feet square, but so what. It was mine. It was awarded to me by my mother because of my being compulsively tidy, and my messy little sister Rebecca got to share a room with my messy older sister Luz, lucky them. It looked as if it had been looted in there and somebody never found the good stuff.

My room had a green shag rug from the bygone days where most of our stuff comes from, and a blue bedspread ditto. So I'd painted my dresser, and the shelves where I keep my trash, alternating shades of blue and green. And that was my room, period, no room for a desk so I did my homework in the living room or bathtub depending on if I had to write something. Oh, blue and green curtains, of course, to cover up the no-view, and the ceiling is approximately a city block high, crosstown. The floor was occupied by my luggage, which I had to step over. A duffel bag for my clothes, such as they were, a bag for half a ton of summer reading, and an airline bag for my shampoo and baby lotion and all that. I had cleverly packed everything—I hoped it was everything—the night before because of how I am in the morning.

I went into the kitchen, where somebody had left me a glass of juice. Drinking grapefruit juice first thing in the morning is such a painful experience that I do it every day in hopes it will wake me up. I don't know if it does, but then, where might I be without it? Then I went into the living room to pull myself together after the shock of the juice. The room was pretty, due to Mom's ingenuity. It was not top luxury, like some of my friends, because Mom couldn't afford it, but it was stylish. And there were a few good things from Grandpa's family home, which helped.

I dragged all my stuff out by the front door, and my older sister, Luz, appeared. If Rebecca is outrageous, Luz is the opposite. It's not in her nature even to understand what outrageous is. She stood there looking like always, the lush, melting-eyed Latin beauty, all gloss and curves and not too smart. She had a scarf tied around her head, tight pants, and a little scrap of tee shirt over her luxuriant chest. She said, "They're down in the car. If you're ready, we'll go, and I'll lock up."

"I'm ready." I got in the elevator and held it while she locked.

When she got in, she said politely, "Are you feeling better today?" She's always polite, except for those occasions when she's hysterical.

"I'm fine," I said, sounding unnecessarily nasty. I really hate it when I'm nasty. I tried a smile even if it was early. I said, "You guys were nice to do all the work."

"That's all right. We didn't mind."

Nice, I thought. I ought to be nice, that's what Luz is. She can't help it if she's dumb and nice. She can't help it if she's prettier than me. Neither can I.

We got to the street. Mom was there looking worried. She always looks worried when we're setting out in a car. Like Luz, she always looks terrific whether she's worried or not. "Good morning, how are you?" she said, and I told her I was OK. She knew not to press it. She showed me where to put my stuff in the car. As usual when we went to the island, the car was loaded to the top and bottom so there was hardly any room for the people. Rebecca was settled in a little nest of boxes and bags, doing a crossword puzzle and blowing bubble gum. We got in and started off. Mom put on her big dark glasses, which she needs to see, since she's very nearsighted. It was a rented car. Whenever she has to have a car, she rents one. Some boyfriend who was an economist or something told her that in her situation, renting a car was the thing to do, so she picked up the information and moved on to the next boyfriend.

Nobody said anything for a while. Mom doesn't like to talk much when she's trying to get out of the city. Even on the parkway we were still quiet. Maybe it's because we were older. Or else maybe it was because of me. My problem was that I was supposed to be in Europe. There was this new thing that year at school, a Junior Achievement Award, and it was a trip to Europe. All year I'd thought I'd win it. It never crossed my mind I wouldn't, because the next best overachiever in the class had moved to Saudi Arabia, a good place for her. And then in the end it turned out they didn't mean real achievement like in grades, they meant good intentions or some such utter crap, so it went to a scholarship girl who was black. They said it was because she was a gifted artist, and she was, she could do every kind of art you could think of more giftedly than I, but I was still bitter. So I got the flu and was still recovering. My mother thought it was psychosomatic. She always thinks everything is psychosomatic and won't take no for an answer. So I was on my way to the island, and everyone was nice, which could be expected to last another twenty minutes, and then I'd have to start getting my own juice again.

I loved the island; it was very soothing. I just hadn't expected to be there until after Europe. The only hope left was that I might meet some boys. I knew all the regular ones, but the guests were sometimes interesting.

"Maybe you'll meet some boys," Rebecca said to me suddenly. She's always reading my mind, maybe because it's often not very difficult to read.

"It'll be just the same old crowd."

"Yeah, Garbage Dave, the McGowan boys, Ratchett and those."

I glanced over at Luz, who was twenty and wore an enormous engagement ring. She was supposed to marry this rich guy I'd only met a few times, but she was also working as a model and liking that. There was no date set for the wedding, but it didn't matter with the size of that rock. Luz said, "I hope we can find good mussels again this year."

"I'm not washing them," Rebecca said promptly. "I don't like having to wash something sixteen times, especially some shell, and then eating sand anyway."

"You haven't washed them since you were seven," I said.

"Well it was a traumatic childhood experience. I'm not sure I like mussels anyway. They have fur on them."

"Oh, Rebecca, they don't have fur at all," Luz said.

This was typical, Luz not understanding when Rebecca was deliberately being horsey. "Yes they do," Rebecca said, typically making it worse. "They have little fur hats and booties."

I thought about the times we had gone musseling. The water always got cold when you stood in it for a long time, and you had to wear sneakers, and scrape the little buggers off the rocks, and it took ages to get very many, and they were heavy to carry back to the car. But then you got to eat them, sand and all.

Mom finally chimed in. "Who remembers the combination of our box at the Post Office."

This was the line she used to drop when we were fighting in the car. Now everybody remembered.

Luz said, "I wonder if Red will still be there. He keeps threatening never to come back." Red ran the fruit and vegetable stand.

"His father and his grandfather used to threaten never to come back too," Mom said. "For three generations they've been saying this is their last season."

"Is Red Italian?" Rebecca said.

"Yes. His Grandfather had red hair, so they called his successors the same name, even though they didn't have red hair."

I remembered the routine of going to Red's, and how it was the thing to bitch about his prices; and he in turn carried on about how rough things were. I had once thought a long time about stealing a plum but decided against it. All those old island memories. I began to get a little stir of excitement. "Let's have another fantastic French picnic, with quiche and wine, on the beach. No hot dogs and hamburgers," I said.

"Yes, and that famous French dessert, popsicles," Mom said. "You ate about twelve that day. That's why you liked the picnic."

"No, I liked the picnic because of your boy-friend."

We all groaned. Some guy had come up for a visit and turned out to be a real loser, and we had had trouble getting rid of him.

"I'd forgotten about him," Mom said. "He really was dreadful. I met him through the agency."

"You got him through an agency?" Rebecca said.

"He had some odd name, too, that I can't re-member," Mom said.

Rebecca said, "It was Herringbone Saddleforth."

"No, it wasn't," Luz said. "Don't be silly."

"But he wasn't as bad as that actress. The one with twenty-four children and a nervous breakdown," Rebecca said.

We all groaned again, and Luz said, "It was four children. I should know. I babysat. And only one of them was hers, isn't that right? The rest were her hus-band's?"

"No, her sister's. Her sister was sick as I remem-ber. She's fine now," Mom said.

"The one I liked was the writer," I said. "The one we were afraid would croak because he turned green and started to pant every time we had to walk more than six yards."

"He must have been before my time," Rebecca said. "I don't remember the green panter. Mom, why do you always invite so many weird people to the island?"

"Well . . . I suppose it's just habit. My parents always invited people, and I guess I just got used to having a crowd around."

"Did Grandpa Will and Paula have weird friends, too?"

"They weren't all conventional. In a way it's too bad they've given up asking people, but it's just too much work for Mother, without help."

"Yes, they're always alone now, aren't they," Luz said. "Like just this time."

Mom said, "I'm sure Grandpa Will and Paula will have left the house perfect for us. They always do, of course."

"I wish they hadn't left," Luz said. "I know they think we like to have the house to ourselves, but I like having them there."

"I think they might have stayed on this time, except that since his stroke Will has to keep going back for therapy."

We were quiet again, probably all still thinking about our grandparents. We have a great-grandmother, too, Grandpa Will's mother, but she's completely out of the picture. I associated the island a lot with my grandparents. They'd gone there, too. Will's mother had built the house when Will was a teenager, and it was really beautiful, but it was meant to be run by a bunch of servants. We didn't have a help problem; that's what everyone called maids, help. We had a money problem. Amongst others.

2

I looked at the back of Mom's head and then out the window. I wondered why it was that she managed to give the impression of not having quite worked it out as a grownup yet. She was mature and very efficient and talented and a good mother and everything, but she somehow had never seemed to get her own life sorted out for more than a little while. She had kept the name of Kristin Kellogg because she's an actress and the name works OK, and for a few other valid reasons. She's not famous but she's done pretty well; and when she works, she makes good money, especially in the TV soaps. But she never feels secure about money because she never knows how long she's going to be working, or how long she might have to wait for the next job, or what will happen if she gets sick. It's a tough, nerve-wracking, competitive business. She works long hours, and yet it's bad to be tired. Also there's no time she can feel really comfortable about money because she has to save for when she's not working, and for Rebecca and me to go to college. At least she didn't have to pay for Luz to go, because she didn't want to. Luz had just about become self-supporting, and that must have been some relief, even though in a way Mom hated to see her in a nerve-wracking career like her own.

Mom has a nice figure, nothing spectacular, just good. She has a lot of auburn hair, which I really think started out that way, and pretty hazel eyes that are always filling up with tears. Her face is what you'd call sweet, although she plays bitch parts very well. She probably looks in her thirties, although I think she's about forty. Maybe even older. We kept trying to date things back, but she kept changing the year things happened. But aside from her career, which I was used to, the interesting thing about Mom was her personal life and how it hadn't worked out.

When she was very young—that's one of the things that kept changing from twenty-one down to seventeen—she was engaged to a guy by the name of Terrance Wood. In fact she'd known him all her life, from summers on the island. His parents were friends of her parents, and it was all really suitable. It was exactly the way it was supposed to be in their social set. They had real social sets in those days.

And then she did this weird thing that really doesn't sound like her at all. She met a Latin waiter, at somebody's coming-out party or some such event, and ran off with him. Really. And it was said they got married. And then it was said they got unmarried. It's hard to get her to talk about it. Whatever happened, she came home after a couple of weeks all upset because he'd left her and gone back to Nicaragua or Costa Rica or wherever he came from, and there was some question about whether or not he already had a wife when he so impetuously whisked her off, and the whole thing was pretty exotic. But it cooled off, and she was taken back into the fold of the upper class, which sounds as if it wasn't entirely unused to scandals anyway, and it was all as if it had never happened. Except for one thing. She was pregnant with Luz. So the little bit of girlish nonsense couldn't be laughed off so easily as it might have been.

However, oddly enough, Terrance Wood hung in there, and I guess he told her that if she would promise never never to run off again, they could still get married, and he would raise her black-eyed little girl as his own. So they did get married, as soon as she could fit into a wedding dress again. And Kris and Terrance had me, and I look like him; I certainly don't look like her. His parents were so teed-off that he married her under the new circumstances that they moved away from the island, and I have never even met those grandparents. But then, while I was still a baby, Terrance died in a car wreck. He was survived by Kristin Kellogg and Luz Muñoz and Cecily Wood. He didn't leave her very much money.

At that time, Mom's dad and her grandmother were able to help her a little bit, but even so she felt she had to work, so she stopped playing around with acting and went into it seriously. It was lucky she did so well because she really needed the money after a while. But then, she's the kind of person who's willing to work very hard, so if acting hadn't worked out, she probably would have done fine in something else.

She next married Auden Grau, who was smart and funny and all sorts of good things. Except one. He was a drunk. She stayed with him for a few years because she loved him and didn't like the idea of being a three-time loser, but once she was really sure he wasn't going to reform, she left him. She said she just couldn't put herself and us through that kind of life. That experience slowed her down for a long time. But she had Rebecca, of course.

Auden was about the closest thing to a father any of us had had, and even after he split, we all still kept seeing him. He was nice even when he was drunk; he was never mean, but it was embarrassing to have him fall asleep in the soup in restaurants and fall down the subway steps. Then Mom made a rule that he wasn't ever to show up drunk or even drink when he was with us, so that cut his visits way back for a while. Finally, I guess he got the knack of staying sober for limited periods of time, because he'd been coming around pretty regular for a year or so. He'd been taking us all out to Sunday breakfast or lunch almost every week because usually nobody worked then. So we had decided he must be a little better off financially, too. I think for a long time he hadn't helped Mom out with money at all because he wasn't working. Although we'd all heard he was supposed to be very gifted. He is connected with TV also. Rebecca was very philosophical and adult about Auden, but then she could afford to be. She was the only one with a sort of living presence as a father, occasional as he might be. Luz and I might just as well have been brought by the stork, and maybe Luz thought she was.

So we were in this situation, and it was no big deal. We were all used to it. However, there was my mother. She really did give the impression that she was just a long time in doing the usual thing—settling down with a permanent live-in husband—and that soon it might happen. She was not dependent on men, and she had a lot of friends, but you still got the impression that she didn't feel as if there was anything permanent about how things were. You couldn't blame her, considering what had happened so far, but it was nerve-wracking anyway. Each guy she brought home, we wondered, is this going to be old Dad. Very often there was something wrong with the guys, at least in the role of old Dad. She always said they were just friends, but we were never quite sure. I knew she really did know a lot of men who were just friends, and maybe we'd gotten super-sensitive on the matter. It had been a long time between husbands, and we were all afraid she was due for another one at any time. It couldn't matter as much to Luz, as she was about to have her very own husband, but Rebecca and I rather liked things the way they were. Still, we wanted to see Mom helped, to see her have somebody to share with and not have to worry so much about her work and her future. So we were a little uncomfortable part of the time. And now she had a new guy. His name was Gene McDermott. He'd only been around twice to pick her up so we didn't know him. Except for a really horrible Midwest accent, we couldn't see anything wrong with him so far. He did call us "young lady," which was pretty unforgivable, but one had to learn a little tolerance in such matters.

We were getting close to the town where the ferry leaves from. I started getting the old excited feeling again, the same as always. We hadn't been there since the summer before. Mom had been busy and hadn't been able to get away, and my Grandparents hadn't been able to go because of Will being sick. Each time the three of us girls had thought about staying there alone, we had decided against it without even bringing it up with Mom. Luz couldn't stay long because of work, which would have left Rebecca and me, and we had agreed we would be spooked out alone in that big old house.

When we were little, we sometimes went for Thanksgiving or Christmas, and there were visiting friends of everyone's, and it was nice. It is a huge house, but it certainly isn't unusual for where it is. A lot of people built huge houses on the island in the twenties and thirties. They all have nine bedrooms and five bathrooms and a couple of sitting rooms and kitchens with pantries. People used to have their staff come and open it up at the beginning of the season and close it at the end. We used to have help when we were little, and there were old island stories about them, too. My Grandmother had a girl whose lover was living in the house the whole summer and Paula didn't find out about it until the end of the season. One season she had a man who was very good except he had a habit of disappearing.

As soon as we were in the town, Rebecca started bouncing around in her seat. Luz smiled and looked around, instead of at her fingernails and her diamond, which is what she'd been looking at most of the trip. "There's the ferry." Rebecca started making little yipping noises.

"I wonder if it's the same crew," Luz said musingly. She had always attracted a certain amount of attention amongst the crew, most of whom were young guys. We lined up where the cars were supposed to go on, and Mom immediately saw people she knew who were also waiting. The Captain said hello Miss Kellogg, which is what everyone called her regardless of husbands; who wanted to keep memorizing new names? We got on the ferry, and the whole bit with the circling gulls and the salt air and the sea breeze was just the same as always, no magic was gone, it could never change. Mom spent the trip talking to the people she knew. I could hear them catching up on the news. Old Dr. Driscoll had died; the Turnbulls had sold their house to the Gerety's daughter, what was her husband's name, wasn't he related to the Turners. And were the Renfrews coming this season; someone said Mrs. Renfrew was too ill to travel, and Chippy French was going to open the house again this year and so on. I gradually turned it off. It sounded a lot like last year's news with the names changed. Luz was posing over the rail, and Rebecca was talking to some kids. I just sat there hoping for an instant tan and wondering what I would be doing in Europe now. Still, I forgot it when we reached the island, and people were calling out to each other and carrying on. Nobody was meeting us this time. It was nicer when Paula and Will were there. We got back in the car and drove off the ferry, through the tiny little town that always looked the same. Then on down the main road, which wasn't even paved when Mom was our age, and then off on the side road where our house was. Rebecca was doing her yipping act again and carrying on a little monologue. "Oh look, the gulls are still having a convention on the driving range, look at them all lined up waiting for the speaker . . . look, the ospreys are back in their nest, I think they brought a bunch of house guests this time. . . . Somebody has cleared that place, did you see? That used to be a jungle. I wonder if they're going to build, I hope not . . ." And so on. And then, "Here's the driveway . . . Oh, there it is!" We all giggled, partly at Rebecca's enthusiasm, partly because it reflected ours, which we were too old and dignified to express the same way. Mom got out and unlocked the door—the last time it would be locked or unlocked until we left—and we all just had to go through the house verifying our memories before we unloaded the car. The house was gorgeous, its wide wings spread out, its big rooms as entrancing as ever. But . . . no, it wasn't exactly the same as I'd remembered it. As I strolled from room to room, letting all those childhood feelings drift over me, I realized that what had happened was that the things in the house had gotten older, just like me. The big old rattan chairs and tables that we used to make houses out of in the play-room were chipped and bent. The ceiling had stains, the floor was scratched. The big mirror in the hall was brown and funny. The wallpaper in the big dining room, with its maidens and gentlemen frolicking in bowers, was peeling. The pretty yellow rose-pattern fabric in Paula and Will's bedroom, which my Mom used, was faded and torn. I had a funny feeling. I hated things to change, but now that they hadn't, all it meant was that nobody had had the money to fix up the things that had worn out. And everything had. Well, anyway, it was still great. I went to get my luggage and put it in my room.

3

We'd decided on our rooms weeks ago—I was supposed to move into mine when I got back from Europe, but never mind, I was moving into it now. We didn't always have the same rooms because it depended on what guests were coming. This time the three of us took the three best bedrooms, the ones along the hall next to Mom's. By the time we'd unloaded our junk from the car, we were ravenous because it was really late for lunch. We took it to the beach, sandwiches Mom had already made and packed back in New York. She does things like that, thinks ahead.

We walked on the beach. I noticed that I had been thinking of Rebecca as a pudgy little girl, but she wasn't. I just hadn't noticed her lately. She had a figure, too. Did she have it last year? I couldn't remember. I had been too busy thinking about myself last year. I suddenly thought, Oh God, I hope she doesn't get too mixed up in those beach parties where they drink a lot of beer and smoke dope and wander away in couples. They generally do start that stuff at about thirteen here on the island. And then I thought I was thinking like a parent, which was ridiculous, and besides Rebecca is a very sensible person. Luz of course looked luscious in her bikini and had for years. Mom looked like a good-looking older sister maybe, or anyway not the mother of that adult-looking brunette. And me. I felt undressed, unfinished, and unkempt.

The sun wasn't too hot, so Mom didn't make us get out of it in half an hour the way we had to when we were little. We left when it was time to go home and start dinner. Before we ate, we all sat in the living room, and Mom and Luz had a glass of white wine. Rebecca sat on the floor drinking Coke and playing solitaire. I felt at a loss. I had my ton of books but didn't feel like reading. Mom said, "Would you like a glass of white wine?"

"No thank you," Rebecca said, pretending it was she Mom was asking. "I'll have a frozen daiquiri." That was something out of Mom's past that she'd heard about; I don't think she ever saw one.

"Mom was talking to Ceecee, Rebecca," Luz said. Poor Luz. She really never knew what was going on.

"Is the wine very dry?" I asked.

"Oh wow, get that," Rebecca said. "It's the same old rotgut she always drinks, as you very well know."

I wasn't really wondering if the wine was very dry, I was wondering if I was invited into the club. The formal cocktail hour. We all often had wine on special occasions with no respect to age, like the French, but maybe this was my invitation to be a regular. I decided to join them. But then we had to go make sure the asparagus wasn't burning up, and dress the salad, and then it was time to sit down to dinner, so I missed my chance for a family style drunken orgy. We ate in the main dining room. There's a little one, too, originally meant for kids. Mom lit candles. It was nice, and it was good. Luz had done most of it. She often did; she'd suddenly become very big on helping Mom, and seemed to like it. Afterward Mom settled back to say something; you can always tell when she's going to.

"There's something I haven't mentioned yet, because I didn't want it to be the sole topic of conversation for hours. Gene McDermott is coming tomorrow with his two sons."

"Tomorrow!"

"How old are the sons?"

"Do we have to move out of our rooms?"

How long are they staying? What ferry are they taking? Have you met them? When it died down, she said, "I haven't met them. Clem is eighteen and Jay is fifteen. They plan to spend a week or so, but it's open-ended and some or all of them could stay longer."

Another stream of questions: Where do they live? Is Gene divorced or what? Are they bringing their car over? Where do the boys go to school? Mom stayed very cool, which she usually is when she's in control; she only gets teary when she's not. "Gene came from the Midwest, but he's moved East and I met him through friends. He's divorced. Clem just graduated from one of the prep schools, I don't remember which."

"You're really taking a chance, inviting these dudes here for so long without knowing them," Rebecca said.

Mom shrugged. "I can't believe they'll be horrid. I never answered your question about your rooms. You don't have to move. We'll give them the old servant's rooms off the kitchen."

"Are you going to marry Gene McDermott?" Rebecca asked. She was the only one who would have asked.

"I have no plans of marrying anyone," Mom said, as if she were answering the press.

"If you do, we'd have brothers. Can you imagine brothers!"

"Well don't stand around on one foot waiting for brothers," Mom said.

"If you did decide to marry him, you'd give us plenty of warning, wouldn't you? I mean you wouldn't just pop off and do it."

"Of course not!"

"Well there's no special 'of course not' about it. I mean you did it before three times."

"I don't appreciate that sort of remark at all, Rebecca. You were not around when any of my marriages took place, so don't pretend to a knowledge of what happened, or make judgments and offhand nasty comments about what you don't understand."

This did not hurt Rebecca's feelings. It only deflected her. She said, "Are we supposed to call him Gene? Or Mister? or Sir, or Man . . ."

"Call him Gene."

Luz said, "Mom, what sort of work does he do?"

"He's a banker."

"A banker from the Midwest! How square can you get. I bet he says 'heck' and 'gosh.' "

Mom's eyes were flashing. "Undoubtedly you will find him square. You make me very grateful I spared myself hearing all this nonsense until now. And I hope, in your infinite wisdom and experience, you will elect to treat this man as a human being, and not as someone whose every attitude you think you already know."

"Yeah," Rebecca said. She was finally a little bit abashed. After a while Luz asked again what time they were coming, and Mom said five o'clock, so we'd at least have the day without them. We got up and cleared off the table and cleaned up the kitchen. Now that the news was out, there suddenly seemed little more to say. So we said little more. We went our separate ways with our books and projects. Luz went in to talk to Mom a while; but I was sleepy and went to bed early.

"I hope you understand why I can't discuss my work with you," the young Englishman was saying.

"Of course I understand."

"It would be dangerous for us both for you to know any more."

"I realize that, Robin," Sophia said. She smiled at him and lifted her mug of ale to her lips, then put it down on the heavy oak table. This was such a pretty inn, nestled away in the country, it was odd to be discussing his dangerous work. She said, "Actually, you know very little of me."

He lifted his blue eyes to meet her gaze. "I know enough to know I want to know more. It's been lovely these past few weeks."

"Yes."

"Oh God, if only things could be different," he said in an anguished voice. "If only we could live like normal people, and stay together like others."

"Yes, but we're not like others," she said.

He gazed out at the gently rolling field beyond them. "Perhaps you are the braver of the two of us," he said. "Perhaps you should be doing my job."

She only smiled.

"Sophia, you're not ... in my sort of work are you?"

"Let's not talk about work," she said softly. "We have so little time left. . . ."

4

I woke up the next day and rushed instantly to confirm the morning view. There was none. You could barely see the trees beyond the lawn, much less the water beyond that and the towns across the water. We were having one of our island fogs. Sometimes they clear by noon, sometimes they don't but it doesn't matter to me because I love the fogs and rain almost as much as the sun on the island. Then I remembered something—a boy was coming and my heart sank. Boys are very interesting but not so close at hand. He'd probably fall in love with Luz and spend the entire time mooning over her. Or else if he was sort of, well, not too tall and heavy, not a big jock either, medium studious and nice, maybe I could actually get along with someone like that. The fact was that I was a little bit afraid of boys. They seemed big and aggressive and confident. Even the small ones and the quiet ones and the creeps gave the impression of having some kind of confidence. I think it's because they know they're in charge of the world, even if they do think they may have to divide it up with the women someday. It's not that way now, and it must do something for a person to know he is the sex that has always ruled the world. Not that they've done such a hot job of it. Maybe we wouldn't do any better, but we don't know yet.

I had a rotten history with boys. My first real boyfriend was on the island when I was thirteen, this ordinary guy who wasn't too scary and I liked. But all he really wanted to do was as much sex as possible, which I didn't want to do so we spent a lot of time wrestling around on a blanket on the beach and scrambling in the sand. It was OK, it spiced up that summer, and I've seen him around since but don't think much about it.

After that there had been a few boys I'd liked, small mild boys, and I wrote letters with some of them for a while, but they went away to school and it's hard to keep up a very heavy passion when all you see of each other is at dances a few times a year. But the worst failure had been the year before. I had been madly in love with a guy named Dave, who worked on the garbage truck, and nobody could understand why I was hanging around the garbage all the time. Working on the garbage truck doesn't have the same significance on the island it does some other places because a lot of the rich summer people do it. At first it looked as if it were really going to turn into something, and then he fell in love with somebody else, the same girl all the summer regulars fell in love with that year. She was an *au pair* somebody brought up, and her name was Alissa. It was true she was gorgeous and even seemed quite nice, although I never got to know her well, but I didn't see why someone was jackass enough to have a person like that messing up my personal ecology, someone attractive beyond all reason. It took her all summer to decide which one she wanted, thereby using up the entire supply of boys, and when she did it was Dave. So that's how my romance ended.

It never seems to be my luck to get into a crowd of plain girls, where I'd look outstanding. I always get stuck with the upper two percent of raving beauties. Anyway, whether it's because of my not having a father around, or brothers, or going to an all-girls school, or living in a city where you have to be careful or what, the net result was that I hadn't had the experience with boys you're supposed to have had at my age. It was nerve-wracking. It was terrible. My only successes came through good old Sophia Scarlotti, who did all my practicing for me and made all my hits for me. Of course, Sophia dealt with more exotic types, not the ordinary boys I knew. They were too hard to deal with. Anyway, right at that moment, what it all boiled down to was that

I hoped I wouldn't have to cope too much with the eighteen-year-old Clem. The idea was awful. Maybe I could start with the fifteen-year-old, he might be easier.

When I went down to breakfast, Rebecca had left for the club to try to stir up a tennis game in the fog, and Mom wanted to do some things in the house but declined our help, so Luz and I went musseling. Luz never talks very much, so at least she isn't disagreeable company, though she's not very entertaining. It was quiet for so long while we were bending over the rocks looking for blue shells that I decided I ought to say something, preferably something about her. I finally said, "Do you miss Parkes very much?"

She looked up from the bucket. "Yes," she said. "I think about him all the time." I was astounded. I never would have guessed that. She said, "And I don't even know when I'll get to see him again because he doesn't really know when he'll be finished making the film he's on."

So Luz had been sad, and I hadn't known it. I said stupidly, "Well, I imagine he misses you, too."

"Not so much, because he's busy. And he's surrounded by girls. Girls always like Parkes. I just hope he doesn't get into some kind of real involvement with one of those skinny blondes. Some intellectual thin blonde."

I was stunned. I'd had no idea Luz thought along those lines. A round brunette scared of skinny blondes, just as vice versa. I said, "Well gee, I always thought people who were engaged could have some sort of . . . trust in each other."

"Yes, of course, and I trust him, but the reason I don't want to set a wedding date yet is I want to give us plenty of time. I mean, I would hate it if . . . anything happened."

Well, I could certainly see what she meant. I guess with Mom's history we'll all feel that way.

Luz straightened up and gazed down into the bucket. "Seven is an awful lot of people to serve mussels to."

"They probably never heard of them or don't like them if they did, since they're from the Midwest."

"You sound like Rebecca." She smiled.

"God forbid."

"One of the reasons I wish I could stay longer is to get to know you better, Ceecee," she said.

That came as another surprise. Poor Luz. Her intentions were always so morally perfect. I didn't know what to say. "It's true our paths haven't crossed much the last couple of years. Our schedules are so different. But you seem very close to Mom, at least."

"Yes. She works so hard, I like to help her when I can. She so much wants everything to be nice for us."

"Yes, I know," I said, although I didn't know what she meant by nice—whether she meant we shouldn't be deprived of something, or if she was talking about Mom's packing sandwiches and lighting candles.

The fog was still with us. We picked up the bucket and went home and ate yoghurt and washed mussels and played solitaire. Rebecca was dropped off after having lunch and another tennis game. We sat around the kitchen table with three different decks of cards, playing solitaire.

Mom emerged from somewhere in a minor tizzy. "Oh dear, it's so late," she said. "I've made up their beds. Luz, would you go to Joe Poldranski's house and pick up the lobsters? I've done such a dumb thing. I spent a lot of time arranging those purple flowers in the three downstairs bedrooms, and now I'm running a little late. I do have the table set, and I've made the dessert except for whipping the cream. Rebecca, would you do that? Ceecee, I'm going to take a bath; would you fix the tomatoes the way you do? And we'll have to leave for the ferry in half an hour. Oh dear. Will Luz be back by then do you think?"

"Sure she will, go take your bath," Rebecca said, waving the egg beater. Mom sprinted off upstairs. "See, she is going to marry him. She's all in a snit. Flowers yet, for two big boys and her square admirer. They won't even notice."

"I think Gene will notice."

"You do? Why?"

"Because I don't think she'd do flowers for somebody she didn't know whether he liked them or not."

"Well, it's too bad you are unable to speak the language, but I see what you mean."

"You've got cream all over your front, Rebecca."

"Want to switch jobs?"

We finished up what we were doing and then went upstairs to do our grooming. Rebecca's consisted of a hurried swish in the tub and the re-doing of her pony tail. I was thinking of putting on a kaftan because I knew Mom would wear one, but lost my nerve. Instead I put on my cleaner jeans and some lip gloss. We ran downstairs, and Mom was standing in front of the door. "Luz isn't back yet."

"She'll be back. Relax."

"We could easily have picked the lobsters up on the way back from the ferry, but I wanted to come directly home."

I said, "They won't fall into a panic if we're a couple of minutes late."

"I hate to have anyone standing on the dock in a strange place wondering if they have the right weekend."

Luz pulled in just then, and we all piled in and took off. I knew I was nervous and I thought Mom was nervous, but I guess we were the only ones.

5

The ferry was just coming into the harbor when we got there, so there was time to park the car and join the smiling throng gathered to meet loved ones. Mom said, "If you don't like the looks of the boys, please smile anyway and give no sign. I'm counting on you." She didn't address anyone by name, but I presumed she meant Rebecca. Suddenly, with no idea I was going to say it, I said, "Call me Cecily. I will not answer to Ceecee any more. From now on you must call me Cecily."

"Really, what a time for a name change," Rebecca said.

"Please," I said. "It's important. Really."

"Yes, all right, I'll try to remember; there they are; the one boy is carrying quite a big dog. I forgot they were bringing a dog."

"That kid with the pimples, that's Jay?" Rebecca said.

"Stop that. Hello," Mom said, turning to a group she knew. "Be nice," she hissed, and turned back to the boat with a smile. They tied up, and the people started pouring off. I'd seen another boy next to the one with the dog, and now he came off carrying the dog. I knew then that he was Clem, and I knew, too, there was no way I could manage him. He was pretty big and fairly good looking, not the type I could deal with at all. Then all was confusion. Clem came over and introduced himself and said his Dad was doing something and then Jay came out; he was as big but much uglier. I was looking as mean as a snake, I'm sure, because I was so put off. We were in a huge crowd of milling people. Clem was saying of his dog, "This is Skipper."

"What a terrific name," Rebecca said.

Clem caught on right away. "Isn't it? It was that or Rex. Maybe Spot or Pal." Gene showed up, and we were trying to get our little gang organized when all of a sudden something terrible happened. The dog jumped out of Clem's arms, and we heard growling and snarling and screams, and then I saw there was a monster dog fight going on. There are always so many dogs on the dock and the ferry, that I wonder why it never happened before, but it happened right then. The dog Skipper picked was an Irish wolfhound, which was a really poor choice for attack because the dog would have stood about nine feet tall if he got up on his hind legs. It was terrifying. Everyone really thought we were watching a murder right there. Finally somebody got them apart, leaving Skipper lying on the ferry dock with all four feet in the air, looking like a ragged toy. Clem looked worse than the dog; he scooped him up very gently and said, "Where's a vet, I've got to get him to a vet right away."

"There's none on the island," Mom said breathlessly.

"Then I'm taking him back to find one," Clem said, and started very purposefully back to the ferry.

"Wait," Gene said. "You don't even know where one is."

"Cecily does," Rebecca said. Imagine that. Even in an emergency she remembered what I'd said.

Everyone was talking at once, Gene was shelling out money as if he were handing out flyers; and the next thing I knew, I was on the ferry with Clem and Skipper. At that moment all I could think of was how lucky I hadn't put on the kaftan, and how lucky I had on shoes, which I seldom did in summer. As we pulled out, I looked back to our little group on the dock, and they were in various stances of confusion and bemusement. I went back into the cabin where Clem was cradling his poor torn dog, and I felt that his well-being was partly my responsibility. I was remembering where you get a taxi, and thinking about how to get to the vet's. Looking at the dog, I didn't feel too sure he was going to make it that far. I crouched down and looked at poor old Skipper. "How do you think he seems?"

"Not too good. He seems weak, and I think he's in shock. How far is the vet?"

"About ten minutes by taxi. It won't be hard to get a taxi at least. Your Dad gave me a whole roll of bills. Do you want to take it now?"

"No, hang onto it, will you. Will the doctor still be there at this hour? I mean, by the time we get there? I mean, the ferry takes forty-five damn minutes."

"They'll get him for an emergency. And the attendant is really good too—she took care of our dog summer before last."

"What happened to your dog?"

"Well it sounds a little ridiculous, but they decided our dog had some kind of insect bites. She was covered with welts and her eyes were shut and she was shaking. But she was fine. She's dead now though."

"Weird."

"Yeah, we thought so. Hey, I'm going to buy our tickets, OK?"

"Go ahead."

When I came back, Clem said, "I still can't believe this. It happened so fast, didn't it? I never thought this dumb dog would do a thing like that. It wasn't the other monster's fault. I saw Skipper go for him. And then all those people got into the act."

"It's lucky all the other dogs didn't get into it. The island has a huge dog population; there could have been a forty-dog fight."

"Well, Skipper's still breathing, but he's not exactly coming around fast." He heaved a sigh, as if he were beginning to adjust to this new turn of events. He finally looked at me as if he were seeing me. "Well it's a new way to start a summer vacation. Going right back before you get to the house."

"I know. It's funny what you think at a time like that. I was thinking how lucky I had my sneakers on, because I'm usually barefoot and then I can't go into the stores."

"I wasn't thinking at all. I would have come over here without a cent. That would have been smart. And I wouldn't have had the first clue about where to go if I was alone."

"I guess you'd go to the cops."

"I guess so."

"You found your way to the ferry dock and everything without any trouble? I don't know where you started out from."

"Well that was another thing. We just bought this house in the suburbs and Dad doesn't know the area at all. So we got lost and almost missed the ferry. And Jay and Dad had a long argument because Jay thinks he's so smart, natural sense of direction you know, and he kept telling Dad when he was making a mistake. I was completely out of it, I have no sense of direction whatever. If I don't know the exit number, I have to go back home and start over."

"Me, too. Hey, you don't have a Midwest accent like Gene."

"No. I've been in the East in school for a long time, and my Mom comes from New York." He looked down at Skipper again. "How are you, stupid? Besides suicidal."

I said, "You knew right away who all of us were."

"Well, I recognized your Mom from TV."

I was waiting to get scared and uneasy, but it hadn't started yet. He was big, but not gigantic. Also I was still wrapped up in our emergency; being scared it would start soon. He was good-looking but not gorgeous. He had quite a bit of brown hair and nice hazel eyes. I said, "Where did you get your tan already?"

"I got it already on the Cape. I spent a week there visiting my old roommate. In fact I was supposed to work there this summer, but the deal fell through. So now I'm one of the unemployed. I won't find a job this late."

"I thought fleetingly of looking for a job. But the jobs here are limited. Especially for girls."

"Why?"

"Well it's mostly hacking away at the underbrush, and I'm not too good at that."

"Yeah."

I could see he was still really worried about his

dog. I said, "Listen, if I can find an empty paper cup around here, shall I get him some water?"

"That would be good."

There were often empty cups rolling around the floor on the ferry going back, and I found one and filled it at the water cooler. Clem offered it to him, but he didn't respond. "I don't think he's going to make it," Clem said.

"We'll be in the harbor in about fifteen minutes."

"Look, why don't you tell me about the island. Can I go snorkeling? Can I get any blues?"

"If they're out there you can." I started talking about the island, just as if he were a girl I was trying to distract instead of a big boy. I told him what kind of fish we had, and some of the fish stories I'd heard. It turned out we both like spearfishing. We talked about snorkeling different places and about scuba and then about sailing, and then we were docking. We got off the boat as soon as they let the gangplank down, and went over and got a taxi. Once in the taxi, Clem didn't say anything, and I didn't either, except to tell the taxi driver where we were going. When we got to the vet's, Clem took Skipper in and I sat in the waiting room alone reading "How to Enjoy Your New Puppy" or some such gripping publication. The fact was that although I was very sorry about the dog, I was more astounded by not being scared of Clem yet, not feeling self-conscious. Then I thought about back home and how they certainly wouldn't have any trouble breaking the ice with all there was to talk about. They were eating mussels and lobster by then. And when we got back . . . and then the thought hit me. No ferry back. We'd just taken the last one. Another problem to solve.

Clem came out looking pretty upset. "She said to call the vet tomorrow. I left him there. She said the vet will look at him, but she doesn't think he's doing well. I could have told her that, the dumb cluck."

"Oh. Well, I'm sorry. But, uh, we also have another problem."

"What's that."

"We just got off the last ferry of the day. No more."

"Oh. Well there must be a place you can charter a boat."

"No, there isn't. A couple of times when we needed a boat very badly, we called on the McGowan boys, but they won't be here for a couple of days yet. Mr. Ratchett would come get us, but it's Saturday, and they will either be giving a party or going to a party."

"Then there's nothing for it but to go to a motel and have an orgy, is there?"

I smiled. "Right. Or charter a plane."

"Hell, I knew you'd think of something. How far is it to the airport?"

"Quite a way. We won't have enough money for the taxi fare and two plane tickets."

We counted out our remaining money and then Clem said, "Well let's worry about first things first. Should we call the airport and see if they're flying? Before we go out."

"I guess we'd better. There's no use waiting there all night if they don't have a plane or if it's too foggy."

"What a mess! And all because my rotten dog thinks he's a pit bull."

"No, it's all because we have our house on an island instead of in a normal place like everyone else."

We went to try to call the airline, and that wasn't as easy as it seems either, because they don't have desks and all the usual stuff at these little airports; but we were told to come on out and there would be a plane back in a while to take us over. Or they thought there would. The other charter company didn't answer. We discussed whether to wait the night in the railroad station and take the first ferry over the next morning, which would certainly be cheaper. We discussed whether to call our parents then and ask them, or call later and tell them. We finally decided to go to the airport and wait for a plane. Then we talked about how to take a flight with insufficient funds, and about if it was too foggy how we'd have to wait for it to clear and so on. But we didn't get mad or upset, which was good, and in fact in spite of everything, none of it mattered a lot to me. It didn't seem to matter to Clem either, and we both figured our parents would understand.

6

The airport was very rudimentary, a lot like the one on the island, which is nothing but a strip next to Tom Cronin's garage, adjacent to the dump. The guy at this one told us he had a plane at the Vineyard that would come for us as soon as the fog lifted there. It took us a while even to find someone to tell us that. He did tell us the price. Neither of us mentioned that we didn't have it.

"Hey, this is the kind of airport I understand," Clem said. "Where is gate one? Where is gate thirty? Where do they take our bomb away from us?"

"They let you keep it, on this airline. Because if you want to go somewhere else, you run out of gas."

"Fair enough. Listen, had we ought to call Kristin and Gene and tell them what's going on?"

"Yes, we'd better do that. They're probably eating the great dinner we're missing."

"Don't talk about it. I'm starving. What was it?"

"Mussels and lobster. Maybe you don't like mussels."

"I'm a nut about mussels. I ate them the whole time I was in Europe last year."

I was glad nobody heard that and hoped he wouldn't say it again. We called home, and they agreed it was better to wait for a plane than any of the other lousy alternatives. So we sat down to wait.

"I wonder how Jay is getting along with two girls," Clem said. "I imagine Rebecca will tear him apart."

"Really? But you don't know Rebecca!"

"No, but Dad told me all about your family."

"But he hardly knows us."

"Right. But your Mom does, and she told him. OK?"

"Well, I guess so. What did he say about me?"

"Not much, just that you're the middle one, Cee-cee."

"Cecily, please."

"OK, Cecily."

"It's funny you've heard about us, because we haven't heard a single thing about you. We didn't know you existed until last night."

"Oh. Then you haven't heard about my . . . family."

"Just that your parents are divorced and that your Dad comes from the Midwest. We could tell that anyhow."

"Well, I guess Kristin doesn't talk to you as much as Gene does to us. Sure, we heard all about her marriages and everything. She's certainly had some bad luck."

"Yes, I guess so." I felt a little uncomfortable for the first time. "If she didn't tell us about you, I wonder how come she told him about us."

"Actually he didn't hear all of it from her. He heard some of it from Mr. Grau, Rebecca's father. He and Gene are old friends. Grau is really a nice guy."

It didn't surprise me that Gene knew one of Mom's ex-husbands. Practically everyone knows everyone in my mom's world. I said, "Grau is a nice guy when he's sober, but he's a pain when he's drunk."

"He's a lot better now, I'm told. Last time I saw him he was really funny. The one in your family I feel sorry for is Luz."

"Luz? Why? Why would anyone feel sorry for Luz?"

"She must feel like some kind of a . . . terrible mistake or something. I mean, your dad was all right, he just died young. And Grau is OK, basically, as a person. But Luz's father, he's just like in limbo. I mean, it must be a weird feeling to have your dad kind of nowhere."

"She's never said anything about feeling like that. Nobody has."

"Well that's not surprising."

"What do you mean?"

"Well, your mother can't very well say much about him or imply that everybody else's father was great but hers was rotten. I don't know. It's none of my business. I just wouldn't like the feeling that one of my parents was ... I don't even know her. I'm sure it's not important."

He was either getting bored or in too deep. I was trying to think of a way to change the subject, but he did it himself. He said, "Do you always go to the island in the summer?"

"Almost always. I wasn't supposed to go there until later. But it ... just didn't work out the way I expected."

"Is it a secret?"

"Not really. I was supposed to win a trip to Europe. I won't go into all the details, but anyway what happened is that another girl got it, a black girl who's a very good artist."

"Oh. Too bad. At least it must make you feel good to know it went to a black girl."

"Why? A black girl is just another girl."

He thought a moment. "You know, you're right. I guess if we really believe everyone should have a chance, we don't need to get all dewy-eyed about any particular ethnic group member getting something special."

I couldn't remember it ever happening before that, before my very eyes, somebody was changing an opinion because of something I said. It made me think I'd better examine my own opinion again.

We talked about schools, and about our friends. We had no trouble talking. I thought I could easily have talked to him all night, and then I was wondering if maybe I was going to. No airplane had shown up yet, and our money hadn't duplicated itself in my jeans pocket. We'd lost track of time. Clem stood up and stretched. "I think I'll see if I can track someone down. I'd hate to have them forget us." He didn't find anyone, but a few minutes later a little plane came in, and it turned out to be for us. Clem was good about the money. Briefly he explained what had happened, and said somebody was meeting us on the other side with the rest of it. The pilot didn't seem to mind. So that part was easier than we expected, and we called home to tell them to come get us. Then we took off for the big ten-minute flight. It was eight-thirty and just getting dark. When we got home, the whole gang gathered to catch up on events of the day. Clem told them about Skipper and said calmly he didn't really think he'd live. Then it was their turn. It was really lovely here, Gene said, and Kris had thoughtfully put flowers in each room (I exchanged glances with Rebecca) and served a delicious dinner with one of his favorite dishes, mussels (I exchanged glances with Luz), and they had all been playing Monopoly ever since.

"It was all incredibly wholesome," Rebecca said.

"Yes, we were just going to read from the Bible before you came in," Jay said comfortably. Maybe funny-looking Jay was going to be a friend for her after all. He did have a bad complexion and fuzzy hair, and he was overweight, but he'd get over all that in time. Clem and I ate our leftover dinner, and it was really all quite enjoyable. Everyone was relaxed and funny, except Luz, who is often relaxed but never funny. I went to bed feeling quite happy that night, except about Skipper, of course. I felt as if I'd already known Clem a long time and we were already friends. At least.

"I hope you like Debussy. If not, I shall change the tape." He poured a glass of sherry and handed it to her.

"Thank you, Doctor. I like Debussy very much."

He looked pained. "Please, Sophia, must you persist in calling me Doctor? Do call me Günter. Unless you would like me to call you Doctor Scarlotti?"

Sophia laughed. "That's not necessary at all, Günter." She looked around the room, his personal drawing room, formal but graceful with its handsome antiques. Outside, the evening light was turning the Alps purple. "I never get tired of the mountains," Sophia said softly.

54

He leaned toward her urgently. "Then please, Sophia, do consider staying on here. After your present assignment is finished, make your permanent home here with me, and work with me at the Institute."

She sipped her sherry. "It's been a pleasure working with you, Günter. I do feel very . . . close to you."

"You must realize," he said, "that I am a very lonely man. Since you came here, I have been happy for the first time in years."

She smiled at him. His blue eyes, so cold most of the time, were now soft and vulnerable. "I have been happy here, too."

"My dear, you are the sort of woman I have always dreamed of finding one day. Do not leave me now."

"I shall have to think about it," she murmured. . . .

7

When I went down to the kitchen the next morning, everyone was there except Clem. He had called the vet and learned that poor old Skipper hadn't made it. Clem was in his room.

Gene said, "Cecily, will you see if you can get Clem to come to the beach with us? It will do him good."

Mom must have coached him about the Cecily bit. I felt a little silly, but it was nice, too. I said, "Sure," and went back and knocked on his door. "Clem? It's me. We're going to the beach. Will you come, and I'll show you where the good spear fishing is?"

"Be right out."

So much for that hard job. I ate breakfast, which everyone else had finished; in fact they were all busy making lunch to take to the beach. We all got into the station wagon and drove to the beach together, but once there, Clem and I walked alone. He had a nice enough body, I noticed—you really can't help noticing in cut-offs—but not spectacular, thank God. Mine could probably be classified the same way. It's OK if you like the type. We didn't talk much at first. I showed him the rocks where we usually go spearfishing, and we went in and took a look around, but the water was too roiled up to catch anything. Then we sat on a rock. Clem started to talk then, about his summers when he was little, how he had to go to camp and didn't like it. He made a funny story out of it, but there was something sad underneath. I couldn't really place what it was. In fact in a lot of ways he wasn't like a kid, more like a grownup. He wasn't as rowdy as a lot of boys his age; he was quieter. Well, anyhow I figured I'd have plenty of time to figure him out. Maybe it was all because of the dog.

But he stayed pretty much the same during the next few days. Those few days were the kind you have to remember forever, because they were so good. It was one of those times when everyone's vibes seemed to be working together. We did a lot of stuff together, the whole gang, but Clem and I were alone a lot, too. We got along well all the time. We never ran out of things to talk about, but sometimes we were quiet. Once I said, "Do you live part of the time with your mother?"

And he said, "I live most of the time at school." Later I realized I'd never heard him say anything at all about his mother.

I wasn't raving keen about Gene, but it didn't matter. He didn't spoil anything at least. He was horsey about acting like another parent on the premises, always onto everyone to take a share. "Jay, take your plates out please. . . . Rebecca, how about unloading the dishwasher so we can put these glasses in. . . . Clem, hang the towels on the line, will you. . . . Cecily I'm taking the garbage out, will you sweep the floor. . . ." On and on. He never told Luz to do anything, because she always did things anyway. She was forever doing the ice trays and making coffee and salads.

Clem and I speared a lot of fish. We had a rule that anything we got had to be eaten, so we had fish chowder and broiled fish and baked fish and fried fish. They finally begged us not to catch any more, but we caught more and gave them to people who weren't having luck. We would all go to Red's and pick out vegetables, and we all sat around in the evenings together for a while after dinner. Rebecca and Jay were getting along terrifically. She was always mercilessly making fun of him, but he seemed to like it; he gave it back to her, and she seemed to enjoy having a resident boy around to boss even if he did look like that. They insulted each other all the time. They played badminton a lot, and we'd hear her yell, "Not into the bushes you dumb cluck. I don't want to go in there where all the snakes are."

"You don't? I would have thought you'd like snakes; you have the same disposition."

They grabbed each other's crossword puzzles away from each other before they were finished and teased each other about what words they didn't get. "I can't believe you don't even know what a Tibetan personage is," she'd say. "I mean I'm aware you're a clod, but your teachers must be clods, too."

"Yeah? How about someone who doesn't know who a baseball great is that has four letters and you already had the R? Really. You've been incredibly sheltered. I doubt if you've met more than five or six real people in your life."

And so on. It got on Gene's nerves a little I think. The rest of us ignored it.

The best evenings were the ones when it was cool enough to have a fire, and afterward we'd go out and walk on the beach. The stars seemed right over us. It was no surprise that they decided to stay on the second week, and I was much happier about it than I would admit. Clem said afterward, "I haven't seen my dad have such a good time for years." He didn't seem all lit up about it, but I didn't pay any attention at the time; I was just glad he was there and everything was going so well.

Then we ran into a bunch of kids on the beach one

day, and they told us there was going to be a big party down at the beach that night, and we should all come. All ages go to these things, from the youngest that can con their parents into letting them go, right up to college kids. Jay and Rebecca wanted to go, and Clem said we might as well too, no use hanging around the house all the time. I didn't want to go especially, those parties are all the same, but at least I'd more or less have my own guy with me this time. Mom and Gene were breaking into the social scene that night too, they were going to somebody's house for drinks. So that evening after the usual parental warnings, we all took off for Shipwreck beach. We had a little trouble persuading Luz to go, and I think she finally agreed just out of loneliness. At first I thought she was being superior, but I changed my mind when she said, "Are you sure it's OK? I won't hang around with you." So we unloaded our junk and food and blankets and settled down with the gathering group. The first person I saw was Dave, but no bells rang. I said, "Are you still doing garbage?"

"No," he said solemnly. "I'm into tree work now."

The next person I saw was Alissa. We all swapped names; it couldn't really be called doing introductions, and people were popping open beer cans and eating and swimming and laughing and yelling and all the things people do on those occasions. The darker it got, the more people showed up. Dave more or less hung around me, to my surprise . . . and Clem seemed to be doing a lot of talking with Alissa. By ten o'clock, which was pretty early, it was absolutely no more fun for me. Luz wanted to go home too, but Jay and Rebecca were having a ball, and Clem said it was still early, so we stayed a while longer. At eleven, Clem said that if the rest of us wanted to leave, he could get a ride with Alissa. I didn't know what to do; but I felt so heartsick about it, I decided we might as well do just that. Before I'd even decided, they went off for a walk, and I was about to burst into tears. They were nowhere to be seen when Luz and I took Rebecca and Jay home.

"Gene and Kristin are probably home playing Scrabble," Rebecca said. "Such a clean-living pair as them."

"I know, it's ridiculous," Jay said. "Any self-respecting middle-aged couple would be having six martinis and drag-racing with the others."

That wholesome routine was one of their regulars, but it didn't amuse me much that night. I went up to my room and tried to reason with myself. There was no use my being surprised or hurt really, because he'd never touched me or said anything. We were just friends; anything else was strictly my imagination. We'd only known each other a week or so, and the fact that I felt we'd gotten so well acquainted and got along so well didn't mean any more than that. It wasn't his problem that he was the first boy I wasn't scared of, and it wasn't his problem that Alissa had walked off with my little romantic interest last year, too. I'd just been stupid thinking we had something going. That was what I was thinking while I was brushing my hair and holding the tears back. Luz asked if she could come in and I said OK.

"That David is quite cute," she said.

"Yes. I thought so too last year."

"He seemed to be interested in you."

"Yes. And Clem seemed to be very interested in Alissa." I was brushing my hair so hard it was beginning to hurt. I threw the brush down and started filing my nails.

"I didn't really know if you cared about that or not. I didn't know if you were just getting along with him, or if you really liked him."

I hated to admit that I really liked him, especially now. I said, "It's just so boring how they all drop dead over that girl Alissa."

"She doesn't like one person for very long, though. I mean, I haven't been here very much, but from what I've heard, it took her all last summer to pick on Dave and then she dumped him."

"Yes, OK, but we only have a week left."

"But the thing is, we'll have a lot of chances to see him again, and she won't. I mean, if you like him enough to bother."

"Well I do like him enough to bother."

"You have time on your side."

She seemed so practical and sensible and nice. It was so embarrassing to have confessed to her that I liked Clem, that I decided I might as well go all out on embarrassment and say something nice to her. I said, "Luz, you are such a good person, and a good sister."

Her eyes filled up with tears, jut like Mom's, and she said, "It's sweet of you to say that, Ceecee, I mean Cecily. Because I feel insecure all the time about practically everything."

"You do? At your age? And being beautiful?"

"Maybe some people think I look good, but everybody, practically, thinks I'm dumb, and I don't think I have any talent. I'm doing all right at certain kinds of modeling, but I can never get to the top; and I couldn't be an actress, I'm not clever like Mom. And I always wonder if Parkes will stay in love with me or if he'll eventually find me boring."

"Oh! I had no idea you felt that way."

"And I never feel sure at all that I'm going to keep on doing all right in my career. I try to be very conscientious, but it isn't just that, you know how it is, it's not the way people think at all. It's glamorous about ten percent of the time, and the rest it's working like crazy just to stay even. And then I sometimes wonder if it's even worth it, but of course it has to be, because there's nothing else I can do. I have to do the only thing I can, and I'm never certain I'm even going to do that well."

"Oh, Luz! I didn't know you felt that way. But really. You should have more confidence in yourself. Don't underrate beauty, because it attracts peoples' attention, and then they find out that you're natural and sincere and kind and loyal."

She wiped her eyes. "That's nice of you, Ceecee, I mean Cecily. I do value your opinion. You're so self-sufficient and smart. But you see, if I have any of those qualities, I feel as if in the world I live in they're not valued. At least not as much as being clever and talented and quick, and accomplishing all those fantastic things."

"Well, I feel insecure, too. About certain things. Maybe it has something to do with not having a father around much when we were growing up."

"Maybe." She looked down at her nails and her diamond again. Maybe they gave her confidence. She said, "At least you and Rebecca know who your fathers were, and people say nice things about them. But... I don't even know what my father looked like, and I've hardly heard a single good thing about him. I mean, nobody but Mom even knew him, and she didn't know him very well. She's tried to say kind things about him, but sometimes I get the feeling she's making them up."

I was stunned. Clem was right, and I'd had no idea she felt like that. I was also shocked. I said, "Mom would never do that. Make things up."

"I think she would. She wants to make up for him

64

being the only bad guy. I mean, nothing was wrong with your father, he just died young. And everyone agrees Auden is a neat guy, and they don't blame him for being an alcoholic. Nobody thinks that way any more, but they do understand that Mom couldn't live with it. So it's all OK except for my father."

"It's funny. I never really thought about it being at all important."

"I guess it's only important if it's you. I mean, I can understand how adopted people must feel. I can see why they want to trace where they came from. Not that I'd want to do that..."

"No. Gee..."

"Well, I'd better get my sleep." She stood up. "I only have a few more days here, and then back to work."

"I'll miss you," I said, and meant it.

She said, "Thank you."

She left, and I turned out the light and looked at the moon. I went to sleep feeling sad, and didn't even feel like calling on Sophia Scarlotti for help. I mean, she couldn't comfort me with a make-believe love when all of a sudden things were so rotten with a real life candidate. I knew Clem wasn't in yet or I would have heard the car. Tomorrow I would have to cope with him on a new basis; and if I hadn't been afraid I'd wake up looking terrible, I would have cried myself to sleep, because suddenly things seemed to have gotten sad.

8

It was raining the next day. Nobody was downstairs. They'd left a note saying they'd gone down to town. So I took my breakfast up to bed and read a book. After a while the telephone rang, and it was Dave. He said, "Ceecee, there's a big party at McGowan's tonight, and all the kids from your house will be going. So why don't I pick you up so you don't have to go home with the rest of them?"

"How did you find out that all the kids from here are going?"

"I ran into them at the Post Office. Alissa's going to pick up Clem, and I guess Luz will drive Rebecca and that other kid. So shall I stop by around eight?"

"Sure, that's fine."

I hung up feeling even worse. Now I would have

to watch Clem having some heavy passion with somebody else, and I didn't know if I could stand it. What do you do when you can't stand something, I was wondering. And I would have to stay acting friendly with Clem so he wouldn't know he was breaking my heart; it would be horrible if he knew that. I got up out of bed and went down to the kitchen and put out all the lunch stuff; and when they came in, I looked all cheery and chipper, and I could hardly look at Clem I was hurting so. What a jerk I was, but I couldn't help my feelings. Clem didn't pay any attention to me at all, he was kidding around with Rebecca and Jay. I didn't dare escape to my room after lunch for fear someone would guess I was suffering, so I agreed to play Monopoly with the younger kids; and then Clem declined to play because he said he was going to his room to read. I said, "Listen, before you disappear, there are plans for tonight, right? Alissa's picking you up at eight?"

"Yeah, right."

"Yes, that's what time Dave said he'd pick me up."

Clem left the room. He left me feeling as if I had a great big hole in the bottom of my stomach. Gene said, "Beach party in the rain tonight?"

"No, it's at McGowan's," I said.

"That's where most of them are," Mom explained. "They have a kind of big barn out in back."

Rebecca piped up. "Everyone can debauch freely there. I feel as if I'm making my debut. I've never been asked before. Who knows why I was this year. Perhaps they're also dipping down into the reservoir of eleven year olds."

"I'm certainly glad they debauch," Jay said. "It would be awful if it were too wholesome for you. What do they do, have human sacrifices or what?"

"Oh nothing original," Rebecca said. "Just the usual beer and cannabis."

Gene looked up from his magazine again. "Really? Here?" Nobody answered him. He said, "Kristin? Do they have marijuana on the island?"

She took the magazine away from her nose and said vaguely, "What?"

"I said, do they have pot, grass, here on the island?"

She hadn't been paying enough attention. She said, "Oh, every year somebody brings some I guess." She was about to go back to her magazine when she finally registered the look on his face. "But hardly any of the kids do it. I think it's gone out of fashion. And certainly they don't have anything stronger. The police know it's not a real problem, and . . . it's mostly all talk anyway."

But Gene was not buying this. He said, "Jay, you're going to have to be very careful. I want your assurance that you will leave if anything like that is going on. These things are so often a matter of being in the wrong place at the wrong time."

Jay was counting his Monopoly money. Very coolly, he said, "I always leave groups where a lot of dope is being smoked. It hurts my myopic eyes."

We all went back to what we were doing, but there was tension in the air. I hoped Rebecca had learned something. You can be candid with sophisticated parents like our mother, but watch out for the square ones; you can't tell them anything or they freak out. She really hadn't had much experience with that kind of parent. Our mother had always seemed totally convinced that none of us would do anything really ghastly, and so far as I knew none of us had as yet. We have had our problems, but Mom has always seen both sides, and she had never had a problem about someone getting all hung up on any kind of dope. I had to keep making an effort not to think Gene was a jerk; after all he was only looking after his kid's well-being, I guess.

But I wasn't really thinking that much about Gene. I was thinking about Clem. Why had he turned off me. Because it was apparent that he had, that he was actually avoiding me. Had he just suddenly fallen for Alissa? Maybe so. I had just suddenly fallen for him. Or had I done something wrong? I was trying to think back. He'd been getting a little quieter even before he met Alissa. Had he really? So my mind kept going around and around with all this garbage, and I lost my fake money to the kids. The afternoon seemed to go on and on. The rain didn't stop either. Then Gene got a call, and he and Mom were invited to a party the next day over on the other side of the water. Someone would pick them up in a boat in the morning. They said OK, and then they said they wouldn't be back until late, would we be all right and so on, the expected parental anxieties. But who cared; of course we would be all right; if they wanted to go to a party they should go. We had to hear how we were responsible for the house and each other, but it finally settled down. They were going out that night also. So all right, big deal. My heart skipped a beat when Clem came out of his room to see if he could help with dinner, and I gave him the worst job. "Yes. You can chop the onions." He didn't look at me or complain. Whether it was different people's tense feelings or the rain, we were all a lot quieter at dinner than we had been. And then we began to leave for our various stunning social engagements, me still as full of good cheer as I could pull off and wishing I could forget the whole evening and even the rest of the week. Every time I looked at Clem, he was looking his nice self, only not at me. I decided to try very hard not to look at him any more.

The McGowan boys' parties don't really start or end, they just keep going on. There are three boys, and they always have friends with them, so the barn is always loaded with kids. Their dad comes out and yells at everyone from time to time but doesn't really do anything, and their mother long since gave up. Todd Ratchett was there as usual when we got there. He was one of their old sailing buddies. Also they had the same two black kids as guests that they'd had the last couple of years.

"Hi, Todd."

"How's it, Ceecee."

"Hi, Chris, Randy."

"Hey Ceecee."

"This is Clem," Alissa was saying. So that was her job now.

I settled down on one of the tattered couches with David and let the conversation rattle on around me.

"Are you going in the race?"

"Yeah, if we have it."

"Yeah, somebody said we're supposed to get a hurricane tomorrow."

"I hope it's better than the last one. Man, all those special precautions, water in the bathtubs, and then it just blew a little."

"It took some trees down, though, and one of them landed on our garage."

"Right, my old man says at the first breeze we're moving in with you."

"Hey did you see Howe on the beach? She was wearing like no bathing suit at all."

"Who bought this beer? I never heard of it."

"Then stop drinking it, it's mine."

"Did you see that guy fall off the ferry?"

"Nobody ever fell off the ferry."

"No kidding, somebody's guest fell off the ferry, McGowan."

"Who was it driving on the golf course last night?"

"Some nine-year-old drunk."

"No, it was Billy Grub, I hear it was him."

"It was probably you, McGowan."

"It was Ratchett."

They went on in this mindless vein for some time, all these future corporation heads. Boys can sound so dumb. I guess girls can too, if you tape them in an unguarded moment. David started talking about hockey teams. I hardly noticed at first that he'd stopped, and then I remembered that he was the type that had to be prodded. I said, "Is that one of the most popular spectator sports do you think?"

"Oh no. The number one is horse racing, and the number two is car racing."

So we discussed those things and went on to baseball and football. I could easily make it from one week to the next without ever hitting any of those topics, but this way it left me free to be utterly miserable about Clem and Alissa, who were listening to someone tell a story. Pretty soon there was a burst of laughter. More people came in. Someone turned the music up and the lights down, and there was a lot of noise. I talked to a girl I used to know who had a lot of friends at my school. I talked to the McGowans' guests. David kept wanting to leave, no doubt to go park somewhere. Eventually Luz took the two younger kids home, and someone said the roads were getting really bad from the rain. It didn't take long for the side roads to get big ruts, so David and I left. He drove very slowly on the main road, maybe he'd had a lot of beer. When we got to my house, he said, "Is your mother home?"

"Yes, and her guest and the kids."

He said he'd see me the next day and left without a struggle. Nice kid. He just didn't appeal to me any more. I went inside and found that Luz and Rebecca both had their lights out. I went to bed, but I had a hard time going to sleep because I kept waiting to hear Alissa's car drive in. Mom came in and went to bed soon after I did. Finally I drifted off.

9

I woke up because there were voices in the hall. I opened my door and saw Gene and Mom just going downstairs. "I had to wake your mother," Gene said. "Clem isn't back yet, and we're going to look for him."

"Oh," I said. "Is there anything you want me to do?"

"No, just go on back to sleep."

I listened to them talking about raincoats and flashlights, and then they left. I looked at the clock. Four-thirty. Wow. I thought, if they're parked somewhere, it's dumb because it's bound to attract attention, staying out so late. But maybe neither one of them has a time they're supposed to be in. Why did Gene wake up Mom? He probably wouldn't know where to look for them, that must be why. He must be pretty worried not to wait for daylight. I turned over in bed and had a huge long cry. Why not? I'd been holding back for a long time. When I was finished, I got up and washed my face. Then I put on my jeans and a shirt and decided to go downstairs to the kitchen. I knew I wouldn't be able to sleep any more, thinking about Clem.

Jay was sitting at the kitchen table playing solitaire. I said, "Hi. Did you just get up?"

"No. I've been up awhile."

"I hear the birds, but it isn't getting light very fast."

"It's still raining," Jay said. "It might not get very light at all."

Everything seemed rather dreary. I said, "I'm sure you know they went out to look for Alissa and Clem." He just nodded. I said, "They may be parked somewhere."

"No. Something went wrong. Maybe they got stuck in the mud. Or they had car trouble."

"How can you be so sure?"

"I know Clem. He doesn't go out looking for problems. And he's not the type that just forgets time, either."

"I guess there's nothing we can do."

"I offered to go with them, but they didn't take me. I think it was silly of them not to because it's possible they'll need to be pulled out of mud."

I stood there for a while feeling dumb. I said, "Do

you want some breakfast?"

"Well if you're making it, I wouldn't turn it down."

I got out bacon and eggs. He started a new game. The rain kept beating down outside. Jay said, "They're going to take the main road down to McGowan's and back, and if they don't find them there, they'll try the beach roads. If they still don't find them, they'll call Virgil Pryor."

Virgil Pryor was the Constable for the island. Jay sounded like an old-timer here, already knowing the names and all. I said, "By now the beach roads might be impassable with all this rain."

"Yeah, I was thinking, even just to get from this house to the road, you might need four-wheel drive if it gets much worse."

I turned the bacon. Rebecca appeared, looking sleepy in her ratty old nightgown. She said, "What an unpleasant surprise, seeing you two here like this. Cooking breakfast, as if it were morning. I have to assume you have gone bananas."

"We are awaiting the return of Clemence McDermott, who is officially missing," Jay said.

"No kidding. You mean he never came home last night?"

"Correct."

"Well is somebody doing something about it?"

"Both resident parents have gone out on a search."

"Jerks," Rebecca said. "They should call Virgil

Pryor. He may not be too bright, but he's got a jeep."

"That was going to be their next move."

Rebecca stretched and came over to grab a piece of bacon. I slapped her hand. "Get out of here. I'll serve you in a minute."

Rebecca said, "Maybe he just, ah, fell asleep somewhere."

"Maybe he just did," Jay said. "I seriously doubt it."

"Could I join the vigil and have some bacon and eggs?"

"You can do the toast," I said.

"Really. I'm not awake yet."

"Do you think I'm awake? Do you remember to whom you are speaking?"

"Oh God," Rebecca said. "Which one is the freak who likes white toast, I forget."

"Me," Jay said. "Your memory would improve if you would lead a more wholesome life." He turned on the ancient radio and nothing happened. "This is the third electrical appliance to zap on me. The coffee maker, the vacuum cleaner, and now this thing that represents all contact with the outside world."

"Everything in this house is at least four generations old," Rebecca said. "And besides there is no outside world today. It's been zapped, too."

"The vacuum cleaner is older than four generations," Jay said. "It was invented in the fourth century

B. C. by a Greek named Vacuus."

"It that true?" Rebecca asked.

"How do I know? I made it up, but it could still be true."

We all heard the car at the same time, and we all ran to the back door. Gene got out of the driver's seat in his polite city raincoat, Mom got out of the other side with her country slicker, and Clem got out of the back soaking wet. My heart sank again. Jay mumbled, "Well, he's ambulatory but not top drawer."

They all came into the kitchen. "It's OK," Mom said in her breathless way. "They were in a . . . a little accident, but he's OK." Clem nodded to Jay and went back to his room and closed the door. Rebecca looked pretty wide-eyed. I probably did, too.

I said, "Why don't you two sit down, and I'll get you some coffee." I figured that was the best way to get the details. They accepted. Jay dealt himself a new game of solitaire.

Gene said, "Alissa skidded off the road into a ditch, hit a tree and hurt her leg. Not seriously, we believe, but she couldn't walk. They were halfway between town and her house up at this end. Clem started back for the doctor, but nobody passed him until he was almost in town, so he walked quite a distance."

"He wasn't hurt at all?" Jay asked.

"I think he's pretty sore, he was a little banged around of course."

"When he got to the doctor's, he was out on another call, and it was quite a wait there I gather. He couldn't get to the telephone in the doctor's office, and he didn't know where there was another one. Evidently there isn't one for public use. We had driven all over and were on our way home when we saw Clem and the doctor loading Alissa into the doctor's car. You couldn't see the car from the road too well, which is why it hadn't been noticed. That and the fact that so few cars even went by."

So that was that. I just stood there by the stove, ready to fill any more orders that came along, and felt sad. All you could hear was the rain, people's cups landing on the table, and Jay's cards. Finally Gene said to me, "Do you know this Alissa very well?"

Oh no. Now he was going to do the parent grill. I said, "No. This is the second summer she's been up here working in the Schaffler house, and I saw her a couple of times last summer."

"You saw her at the party tonight. Was she drinking?"

That wasn't fair! On the one hand I would have liked to see Alissa locked up for life, and on the other, I wondered why he couldn't settle for the fact that anyone could skid off the road in the rain instead of making us all out to be full of bad habits. I knew she'd had a beer; I didn't have a clue how many. I said, "She certainly didn't seem at all drunk when I left."

"Had she been smoking dope?"

"No," I said abruptly. Why couldn't he wait and ask Clem all this stuff. Maybe he would. Maybe he was just double-checking.

Suddenly the telephone rang, startling us all. We all glanced at the kitchen clock. Seven. "Who on earth..." Mom said. She picked it up. "Hello... Mother! Not at all... Oh... Oh dear." Rebecca and I were riveted, and Gene and Jay were looking as if they were trying not to listen. I was afraid it was bad news about Grandpa Will. Mom had her back turned, so I couldn't see her face. She said, "Well look, I can get the eight o'clock ferry. I should be there sometime before noon. Keep calm, dear... yes, I know. Take care. I'll see you soon." She turned back to us. "Grandpa Will has taken sick again, and I'm going to have to go to be with them. I'm sorry, I really have no choice."

"Do you want one of us to go with you?"

"No, I don't. For the moment let's just leave everything as it is, and as soon as I've seen him and talked to the doctor I'll decide what the best thing is."

Rebecca burst into tears and fled the room. Jay gazed after her in astonishment. Now Mom began to get a little tense. She didn't have much time, and she hated to leave anyone upset.

"Tell me what you want me to throw into a bag," I said, following Mom.

She started enumerating. She tried to do an instant

comforting job on Rebecca. She wakened Luz and told her. Like Gene, Luz offered to go with her, but Mom said she'd better go alone this time. For a little while things were in pretty much confusion, but finally Mom took off, leaving the rest of us in limbo. None of us knew exactly what to do next, except to mess around in the kitchen a little bit.

Then Jay said, "Dad, do I remember something about you meeting the Ellisons at the dock this morning? Or sometime today?"

"Oh good Lord, I completely forgot about it."

"Oh good Lord," Rebecca muttered, back in the kitchen and herself again.

"They're supposed to be there at nine. I can't reach them to cancel now."

"Why should you cancel now? I mean the weather is certainly rotten, but the party is at their house, isn't it?"

"Yes. But I wonder if I oughtn't to stay here with Clem, and wait to hear the news from Kristin."

"I assume the Ellisons have a telephone," Jay said. "And there are four of us to wait on Clem hand and foot if he needs it."

"In any event I have to meet them at the marina. I can't just leave them there wondering what happened. Luz, will you drive me? That way you'll have a car here if I go."

"Yes, certainly," Luz said. She had barely caught

on to all the things that had happened so far this morning. Who could blame her. So Gene left, and Luz returned. His friends had persuaded him to go to the party, and here we all were.

10

We picked up the house. There didn't seem much else to do. The rain kept up. I felt terribly sad, too sad to do anything at all. Between Grandpa Will and Clem and the rain, the atmosphere was just too gloomy for words. Luz went upstairs to do some cleaning, and Jay went to his room. Rebecca and I sat in the living room staring out at the rain. She said, "I have a terrible feeling that things are never going to be the same again."

That made me feel even worse. I snapped, "Oh, don't be so dramatic, of course things will be the same. I don't even understand what you're talking about."

"I don't think we're going to have any more summers with Paula and Will, and something's bound to happen to this house if Will dies, nobody has really been able to afford it for years, look at how everything is falling apart. And then we won't be able to come here any more."

I had an awful feeling of dread too. Even thinking about Will dying or not having the house made me want to break into tears. So I snapped again. "Well, things keep changing, it's the way life is, but there's no use going on and on into the future when we don't even know what's going to happen today or tomorrow. Don't look on the worst possible side of everything."

"I have to. Otherwise it will come as a nasty surprise, and I won't be prepared for it."

I may have been about to go on, which wouldn't have been smart, but Luz came in. "I think the house is pretty clean, whatever happens," she said. "When I got up and heard about all the things that had happened, I felt as if I had missed a whole scene out of some awful play."

"You missed two acts," Rebecca said. "There's bound to be a third. Quick, break an arm so we can get it over with."

"What?"

Jay ambled in just then. Luz said, "How's Clem?"

"He's still asleep. We're going to get a hurricane."

"What do you mean we're going to get a hurricane?" Rebecca asked indignantly.

"A hurricane is a—"

"I mean how do you know, stupid."

84

"Once it was determined that the regular radio does not work, I began to listen to the battery-powered radio. And the little voice that comes out of it says we are going to get a hurricane tonight."

We all sat around looking at each other. I said, "I heard that last night, but I forgot all about it."

"I hope somebody at Dad's party hears it before they try to start back."

"By that time they should be able to look out and see it," Rebecca said.

"Were they telling people to make the usual preparations?" Luz asked.

"Yes," Jay said. "Fill bathtubs with water, remove large objects that could fly through the air from outdoors—"

"You'd better stay in, Jay," Rebecca said. "If you started flying through the air, you could knock the whole house down."

Jay ignored this and turned the radio back on. He was evidently going to carry it with him like a good luck charm. Sure, there was in fact a hurricane alert out. We kept the radio on, and it kept faithfully telling us what it knew. The thing was, a lot was said about where it was and how fast it was travelling, but very little was said about what one was supposed to do about it. It was certainly windy outside at the moment. We had a little discussion group about what to do next. We didn't need any groceries, so we decided to get some

85

wood up from the basement in case we might need a fire. Our power had gone out plenty of times without a hurricane. Those of us who had lived in the house were fully confident that the power would go out with a hurricane. We did fill the bathtubs, and we went outside and hauled in the garbage cans and lawn furniture. Then we had lunch.

Clem appeared in the kitchen looking touseled and cheerless. Also as if he didn't have any intentions of discussing anything. So nobody asked him anything. I wondered why this was, because very often when I don't feel like answering something, that's just the time people ask. I decided that in this case, Rebecca would be the only one who would ask, but she was preoccupied with other things. Jay did tell him about the hurricane. He finally said, "I suppose you've got candles and matches." We didn't, and Luz went to collect them. It made me feel like a jerk. Then he said, "Jay, you and I had better see if we can't do something about some of those loose shutters." And the two of them went outside, leaving me more upset than I had been before, which was not easy. It's just terrible to be in love with somebody who doesn't love you, regardless of illness and weather conditions. They came in, bringing the charcoal grill and charcoal. We decided that it really was getting windier. Clem had some tea. I had the impression he didn't feel very well. I was wondering if he would call Alissa, but he didn't.

Rebecca and Jay were always carrying on a conversation. She said, "What will happen if we have a tidal wave?"

"Get wet."

"It would take a really big wave to get up to us here," Luz said. "We're quite high."

"I'm not high," Jay said. Clem didn't laugh at any of this witty repartee. They started a game. After a while Jay got bored and asked if he could look out of the upstairs bedroom windows at the water—the view was better from up there. So he took his binoculars up and looked, and we all stood there waiting our turn because it was a new thing to do in a boring situation. "I don't believe this," he croaked. "The water is full of ferries."

"Let me see, you clod," Rebecca said, and he let her grab the binoculars away. She stared out. "Jeez," she said. "The water is awash with boats. Ha ha. Maybe they're all arks."

"They're probably people just getting their boats to safety," Clem said.

"No," Luz said, without benefit of the binoculars. "I think they are probably evacuating people."

"What about us?" Rebecca said. "Don't we get to be evacuated? Why didn't someone let us know?"

"You're supposed to take care of yourself," Luz said. "I'll call Virgil and see if he knows anything about it." She did, while we all stood around openly listening.

When she hung up, she said, "Well, the last ferry left. Part of the road is washed out between here and the ferry anyway, he said, so we have to stay. But he said not to worry, from what he's heard he doesn't think we're going to get the worst of it anyway."

"He's heard the same we have," Clem said. "It's hard to tell what we'll get."

"I guess we all know the power's off," Jay said. It was.

II

The radio voice changed its mind about when we were supposed to get it; by five o'clock it said it wouldn't be until late evening. We decided we should all sleep in the same room to conserve heat and candles and whatever else we should be conserving. Also the wind wasn't quite as deafening downstairs as up. We began to build a little nest in the living room. Clem and Jay made a fire because it was getting chilly, and each of us picked out a place to sleep and brought blankets, and we brought in the stuff we were going to cook for dinner. All this would have been fun if it hadn't been for all the other junk that was going on. Clem seemed pretty stiff and sore, and maybe he and Jay were worried about their dad. The rest of us were worried about Will and Paula and Mom, and presumably we were, in varying degrees, worried about the hurricane. And I was in addition, although it's awful to admit it, taken up most with Clem.

The telephone had not gone out yet, which it proved by ringing. It was Gene, and I realized I was disappointed it wasn't Mom. Gene told Clem he was not going to be able to get back that night. I had the luck to hear all of Clem's end. "No, I'm OK, really, just still a little battered, nothing important . . . No, I didn't think to, I guess I should have . . . Yes, we have . . . yes, we did . . . yes, it's windy but not too bad . . . yes, we did . . . yes, we will. . . ." And so on. Parental advice and questions. OK, just time-consuming.

Then Mom called. She said, "Darling, did you know there's a hurricane?"

Well, that was the first real comic relief of the day. She'd been so engrossed in Grandpa Will that she'd only just heard what was going on outside. When that was settled, she said, "Things aren't going well here. I think you must prepare yourselves for bad news. But meanwhile please stay inside and just wait it out. You will probably not have telephone service much longer, so we'll just have to wait until all this settles down and we see what's happened to decide what to do next."

So that was that. She sounded very rattled, and she had a right to be, worrying about everyone in her family. We sat around the living room, sometimes talking and sometimes not, until we decided to cook dinner.

I noticed that Clem never looked at me unless he had to, and never spoke directly to me. There was no longer any question of whether or not Clem was trying to avoid me, he really was. If I could pull myself together and look at it objectively, I could say to myself that it was interesting. If he was totally uninterested in me, he wouldn't have to be so obvious about avoiding me. And every time I thought about him, a second later I thought about Grandpa Will and would get this terrible feeling in my stomach that I wasn't ready for him to die. And then I suddenly remembered that his mother was still alive, and it seemed so unfair that he should die first. And I wondered about what really would happen to this house, and about what the financial situation would be. It was always known that "Grandma", who was really Great-grandma, had the money. I wished kids were told more. Sometimes it seemed as if Mom were trying to keep secrets from us. On the other hand, maybe I hadn't ever been interested in family stuff before, except in her personal life, which really was her own business.

By late evening we were all bored with the hurricane, before it even happened. They postponed it again, until around midnight. Clem drank some wine and went to sleep. He still hadn't said anything about Alissa or the accident. Or anything else, really. We took the dishes out to the kitchen and did them by candlelight. The hot water gave out before we were through. Luz played solitaire on the floor for a while, and Rebecca and Jay talked. The wind howled. I listened to Clem breathing and thought about Grandpa Will and Paula. They had always been a part of our lives. When we were littler and needed more taking care of, we used to go stay with them. Sometimes they would come stay with us when Mom was working away somewhere. Paula used to be a singer, and she used to sing around the house and tell us what it was from. Grandpa Will was a painter, and he didn't like to stay at our apartment because he couldn't paint there. Paula and Mom both acted a little bit helpless and rattled sometimes; and the difference was that Paula really was that way, but Mom could always pull herself together. Will was just a nice man. I wondered if he'd ever made any money at his painting. I dozed off. During the night I kept waking up. I listened to the wind howling. At times it was almost alarming. But then I'd go back to sleep again.

Then I woke up and there was no more howling and no more rain beating down. It was grey and cloudy outside, with a stiff breeze. It must be over. I looked around the room and saw Jay and Rebecca still asleep, but Clem and Luz were gone. I went into the kitchen, and Clem was there.

"Hi," I said. "I guess we've had our hurricane."

"Yeah, I guess so. I went outside to see if there

was any damage, and there are trees down in the woods and a few shingles missing from one side of the house, but that's all, as far as I could tell."

"We were lucky then. I wonder how everyone else made out."

"I don't know. People can be incredibly stupid about things like this. I mean—even us. We didn't really pay any attention when the first warnings came."

"No, not really . . . how are you feeling?"

"Not too bad. It wasn't good sleeping on the floor. I tried my room, but the noise was bad and I was afraid the windows were going to bust in on me. I'm OK."

"That's good." He was talking to me at least. I picked up the phone. "Still dead."

"Yes, and the power's still off, of course. Kitchen clock is still where it was yesterday."

"It usually takes them a while to get the power back here. It depends on how many trees are down, I guess."

He stopped talking and just stared outside. After a while I said, "I may get some breakfast. Do you want some?"

"No thanks."

All the time I was fixing my breakfast, he didn't say anything so I went into the living room. "You kicked me, you big clunk," Rebecca was saying.

"I didn't even touch you."

"You did. I know when I've been kicked."

"Then you know you weren't."

I said, "Hey you little jerks, the hurricane is over, and we are still above water with the house more or less intact."

"Oh, terrific," Rebecca said. "All that heavy drama and nothing happens."

"Yeah," Jay said. "She would have liked at least for the roof to blow off."

"I wonder what the bathwater was for anyway? We have five tubs full of it now."

"To prevent typhus," Jay said.

"Oh wow. I'm glad I finally met somebody who knows everything."

"Some people are just lucky."

"Can we drive around and see which houses blew down?"

"I don't know. First why don't you turn on the radio," I said. Jay did, and it was music. Evidently the radio had forgotten all about the hurricane, too.

Rebecca said, "OK, so let's get Luz and make her drive us around."

We did. Everyone wanted to see how the island had done during its most recent and probably least dramatic hurricane. As usual, it took a while to get everyone ready and into the car because people kept losing shoes and forgetting a sweater and all. When we started out, I was surprised to see the road almost dry. "Gee, look at that," I said. "Where are all those puddles?"

"The wind blew them away," Jay said.

"Oh, clever, clever."

"It's true."

I was very aware of Clem. He wasn't talking, but he was trying to maintain a pleasant expression, I decided.

Out on the main road there wasn't anything to see at first, and then we saw the trees down. Several seemed to have been dragged off the road, so work crews must have been out for some time. The road was scarcely damp where the floods usually are, and I decided Jay was probably right, the wind blew the water away. We drove all the way to the ferry dock, and huge waves were crashing against the rocks. As far as we could see, there were whitecaps in the water. We were all impressed. Then we went to the Post Office, and there were a lot of cars there—everyone else wanted to see what had happened, too. Clem went in to the utility company to see when we could expect our power back, and they told him probably late afternoon. Rebecca and Jay kept up their constant battle, this time about whether or not the milk in the store would be sour, and whether we should assume that the whole island would be without power because we were. On the way back home we stopped at the beaches and the waves were all high of course, we just wanted to check. Some of the houses were boarded up, but we didn't see any spectacular damage, just a lot of trees down.

"It looks pretty rough for Dad to be coming back," Clem said. "I imagine the small craft warnings are still out."

"It may calm down enough to cross later in the day," Jay said.

Finally we went home and tried to make things normal again. The guys put all the outdoor furniture and the garbage cans back where they were. Luz cleaned out the refrigerator, which was dripping all over the floor, and Rebecca and I cleaned up the living room and the kitchen. We kept all the candles around in case the power didn't come back when they said it would. Then we had lunch. Everyone seemed to feel a little bit low again. Maybe we'd gotten over our good feelings about surviving the hurricane and now it was just a drag.

We were just halfheartedly cleaning up when we heard a car drive up the driveway, and it was a bunch of kids, the McGowan boys and David and Alissa. I wasn't at all glad to see them. The last thing I felt like was a party, but they were all laughs so I tried to look delightfully surprised. They all trooped in bringing beer, and we started swapping lies about our hurricane experiences.

They talked about the accident, too, sort of as if it were a joke. Clem tried to go along with the gag, but even I could tell it was an effort. It seemed that besides the road being wet and visibility being zero, there was something wrong with the steering gear on the car. Alissa would be fine in another few days, although she came in on crutches, and Clem said he hadn't been hurt at all, which I knew wasn't entirely true. But far be it from me to mess up his hero role or whatever it was.

Then they went back to the hurricane again, and I could tell I'd be hearing about this for many summers to come. How many trees were down, what had happened on the mainland, where it was worse, where everyone was. And then, with no comment, Clem just got up and left. Everyone went right on talking, of course, since people do come and go in a group like that, although I could tell Alissa was paying special notice. I wondered if something were wrong, but didn't dare do anything about it. And I also wondered how long they were going to stay; they were boring me a lot. But they were bored too, and our house was at least a change. When they all started up a poker game, I knew they weren't in any hurry to go on to the next fabulous social spot. So I said I'd join in later, and slipped out to the kitchen. I decided to check on Clem. Just right then and there, without thinking and with all the nerve I could muster, I decided to try to talk to him. I was butting in, and if he didn't like me there wasn't anything I could do, but what did I have to lose. I knocked on the door, and he called out, "Come in."

12

He was just lying on the bed doing nothing, and he seemed surprised that it was me. I said, "I'm sorry if you were trying to sleep. I just wanted to tell you they've started a poker game in case you want to join in."

"Oh. Well, thanks, but I'm really not in the mood."

Pause. "Is everything OK?"

"Sure."

Longer pause. "It doesn't seem OK."

"I'm sorry I've been . . . like this lately. It just . . . can't be helped."

I started getting a little bit mad then, which gave me more nerve. I can't stand it when people play games with me and get sulky or won't talk. I said, "Well look, I thought we started out friends. And then something went wrong, and I don't know what it was, but if

I did something wrong I'm sorry."

He sat up. "You didn't do anything wrong. You've been terrific. I know it must seem as if I've been acting pretty weird. Weirdly. And in fact I've been feeling rotten about it. But I don't think I can explain."

"If you've been feeling so rotten about it, you could at least try."

He gave me a wan little smile, which made me feel a wan little bit better, although I had no idea what was coming. He said, "I guess I owe it to you to at least try. How much do you know about my mother?"

"Your *mother!*" I was completely taken aback. Of all the things I couldn't have guessed, that was at the top of the list. "I don't know anything. Except that your parents are divorced."

"Jay and Rebecca seem to have been talking about damn near everything, and I thought she might have mentioned something to you."

"No. Nothing."

He sighed. "Well it's hard to tell this the right way, because it's easy to give the impression that she's . . . some kind of a bad person or a nut or something, and she's not, she's really terrific. So . . . well, she left my dad a couple of years ago; it's hard to explain why, but it was because she felt sort of . . . oppressed, and she wanted to make it on her own and sort of be her own person. She didn't like the kind of people she had to deal with where we were living, and she didn't want to be a housewife all her life, and Jay and I were pretty well grown up anyhow. And she felt as if her life were . . . sort of, fake, and . . . stultifying."

He looked at me. I was trying to take this in, but right at that second I was also trying to remember what stultifying meant, and I decided it meant, like stifling. At least I was glad he was talking to me about something that seemed very important to him. I nodded very wisely.

"So she came back East, where she grew up. She wanted to be entirely on her own, and she didn't want alimony from Dad or anything like that. She took this apartment in New York, and I've visited her there a couple of times, and it's . . . well, it's not much. I mean it isn't anything like what she's been used to all her life. And I always figured she'd come back. She'd try living alone, and then come back. So when we moved back East, that seemed the perfect time. Dad got a house that's really for a family, and all along I figured that at almost any time she'd come home. So . . . well, Dad took out other women and all that, that's OK, nobody expects him to be a hermit. I didn't pay a lot of attention to his social life. He's a very, kind of proper person, so . . . anyhow, he told me he'd met this actress, and I saw her a few times just out of general interest. And then he said we were invited to visit you here, and I'd just lost my job, and it sounded great to be able to go fishing and all. Three girls was a little heavy, but that was OK too. And when I first met you, we really did hit it off right away. It was as if we'd always been friends. And ... you see ... I've had a lot of girl friends and all that, but they ... it's not that I'm afraid of girls. I'm not saying this very well. Anyhow I got along with you from the start.

"But there were all these little things right from the beginning. When we first got to the house, it was so nice. Your mother had put flowers all over, and then she was always fixing stuff she knew we liked to eat, and even nasty Rebecca was getting along so well with Jay, and everything is nice and pretty and warm. And Dad and your mom get along so nicely, and I had the feeling we were all falling into a great big soft trap."

I tried hard not to gasp. The word really infuriated me. With great control I said, "Actually, nobody here needs to set any traps."

"Oh God!" He really did sound agonized. "I don't mean anyone set it. I mean, we're vulnerable, we set it ourselves, we walk into a nice female environment, and all three of us flip out. Don't you see? We should have our own mother and our own household. Your mother is doing OK in her career and her life, and so are all of you and ... I think Dad is falling in love with Kristin. While my mom is still trying to find whatever the hell it is she's looking for and too proud to come back where she belongs. And if Dad and Kristin decide to get married, I'll feel as if he didn't try hard enough to get Mom back and just wants to be comfortable. And I can't do the same thing. I just can't get into a . . . situation with you. With you . . . I haven't been comfortable with a lot of girls, and it's completely different with you."

He paused, either to think or because he was embarrassed. He was telling me a lot of stuff I couldn't sort out just then, but at least the last part was good news. Without thinking, I said, "Aren't you comfortable with Alissa?"

"Oh well, sure," he said, as if that were beside the point. "I mean, she's good-looking and no pressure and not too smart, and I don't care about her. I mean comfortable with someone I . . . like."

I nodded. He'd pretty well summed up how I felt about Dave. And he'd just told me he liked me, so all I had to do was figure out all the garbage. Here was this funny line of reasoning that turned him away from me. He did seem miserable, at least I had that in my favor. I had a feeling there was something definitely wrong with the way his mind was working on this thing about his mother, but I didn't think I had the words to fight it. Also, I had to take it that his mother didn't really just leave his father, she left the two boys, too. So I had to be careful what I said. It was certainly a touchy matter.

I said, "Well, I can see what you mean, I guess.

Except I'm not sure that our parents . . . whatever they decide about their own lives . . . why we can't make our own decisions separately, apart from theirs."

"That would be terrific, except it doesn't work like that. I mean, people's lives get all mixed up with each other. Like, if I . . . got into a relationship with you, and Dad did with Kristin, it would be telling my mother she doesn't count any more, that we have a whole new family. It's saying it's all OK for Dad and us to forget her."

"But even if you did get a new family, why would that have to mean forgetting her? Couldn't you keep on seeing her, just like now, and having it the same except for the changes in your life?"

"No, because there would be this terrible contrast. Where she's living alone in some lousy apartment, and the rest of us have got this . . . more comfortable . . . arrangement."

This all was beginning to sound pretty far out. I said, "What do you think you ought to do?"

"I think we ought to encourage her to come back."

"But . . . what makes you think she wants to? Wasn't she the one who wanted to leave?"

"Yes, but she's had a while to try it now, and besides it's all different because now we live here in the East."

This was too tough for me, the whole thing. I felt as if I couldn't say any more, because his mother sounded to me as if she'd already made her decision quite a long time ago and wasn't about to change. Also I was surprised he didn't seem to blame his mother for leaving. And if he thought it was all his father's fault, why didn't he resent him for driving her away. Maybe he did and was just covering it up. So here we were with nowhere to go, and it didn't have anything to do with Alissa at all. It had to do with some woman I hadn't even known was any sort of problem until a few minutes ago, a woman I couldn't possibly deal with. After a long time of us both just sitting there unhappily, I said, "Maybe you should talk to her about it. Maybe you could get this settled in your mind if you found out exactly what her feelings really are. Because you have to settle it some time, don't you? I mean, if not now, then later on."

"I've tried, but she puts a good face on everything. She doesn't want me worrying about her, so she says she likes what she's doing."

"Well, if you don't believe her when she says she's OK, then you're never going to get used to things the way they are." It sounded too harsh, so I quickly said, "I mean, you know, get to the truth."

"No, because what she says couldn't be the truth. Not when you know how she grew up and how she's lived ever since. I mean . . . on the street where she lives there are people rummaging around in garbage cans, and junkies. And her apartment is tiny."

This was certainly a suburban boy all right. He should live in the city a couple of weeks, then maybe he'd have a better idea of what people see, and not think his mother was suffering anything so unusual. But I didn't know how far I could press my point. I said, "Listen, Clem, just try out another idea. Maybe this environment is new and different and exciting to her. It is to a lot of people, you know. Maybe she likes being in a cultural center. Maybe she likes not being in the middle class, which is supposed to be so materialistic and conventional and everything. Maybe she really likes her little apartment, just because it's hers, and her job for the same reason. Maybe she feels proud of what she's done. I mean, it's possible you could even be cutting her down by criticizing all that, because maybe that's what she likes even if someone else finds it awful."

"No, it's not what she likes," he said, without offering any evidence, so that was that. I thought he was really pretty far off the track on all this, but what could I say. Maybe I'd already said too much, although he didn't seem angry, just miserable. And anyway I could be wrong. I didn't even know the woman, and already I couldn't stand her. Even so, I felt a little warm spot in the fact that he was willing to talk. For lack of anything better, I said, "Does Jay feel the same way you do about all this?"

"I don't always know what Jay feels, but in general I don't think he's especially sensitive. I mean, he doesn't even think much except about factual stuff. He's practical. He just sort of takes things as they are."

What a great idea, I thought, but I didn't say it. I said, "Then he wouldn't be so upset if Gene and Kristin got married."

He shrugged. "I suppose he'd think that if they'd like to get married, they should do it."

"That's one way to look at it."

"Not until this thing is resolved with Mom."

"Except that a lot of people would think divorce was the final resolution."

"Not always."

So there we were again, stuck. We were both sad, and neither one of us knew what to say. I was thinking he was nuts, which he probably knew, and he was no doubt thinking nobody could understand his viewpoint. That's a thought I would certainly support because I doubt if anyone could understand. I said, "Does your dad know you feel like this?"

"Well no, I don't think so. I mean, I can't talk to him about Mom. And as far as your mother goes, and the two of them, I haven't talked to him about that because I had no idea it could be about them getting married until recently."

"He won't talk about your mother? What about after you visit her and times like that?"

"We don't visit her too much because of her job, and until now our school schedules and things like that.

And even then . . . no, all he'll say is something like, how are things down in the Village. If he even says that."

"It sounds as if he's, well, more or less satisfied that everything is OK the way it is."

"Maybe he is. I'm not."

OK, I decided this was the time not to talk about it any more. I didn't want him to start thinking I was the enemy. And then he said, "It must be boring for you, trying to talk about stuff like this that doesn't even really concern you, with your grandfather sick and other things to worry about."

"No. This is all very important to me. Because I really did hope we could be friends. Because I really do like you a lot. And there aren't too many boys I like."

"Well, if it's worth anything, I guess I like you more than any girl I've ever met. But we can't be friends."

Then the most horrible thing happened; I started to cry. But I jumped up and said I heard a car, so he wouldn't see. And I ran out to see who it was, and to my amazement I really did hear a car. So I went back so he wouldn't think anything was odd, and he was looking out the window. He said, "I'm sorry if I've been rotten, but all this stuff was churning around in my head. I couldn't go out and yak it up with those kids."

"I don't care. I didn't feel like it either."

"I thought maybe you wanted to be with them. David, maybe."

"Not especially."

"OK. Let's go out and see who came in. I hope it's Dad."

It was Gene, and there was confusion while the other kids got themselves together to leave, and Gene told about how rough it was on the water, and everyone was milling around talking. Then the kids left, and Gene and the two boys went back to where their rooms were, and Luz and I picked up the living room one more time. All of a sudden the lights went on. "Oh!" Luz said. "Just in time to cook dinner!"

Just as we sat down to eat, the telephone rang.

13

There was a kind of unspoken understanding in our household about the telephone. Mom got it when she was at home because it might be a business call. Next in line was Luz, for the same reason and because she was older and presumably communication was more important. And so on, so it actually went by age. I looked at Luz, and she was in the middle of serving and nodded for me to get it.

It was Mom, sounding very soft and controlled, and so I had a scared feeling right away. Rebecca had dashed away from the table to pick up another extension—she must have had a feeling, too.

"I'd very much prefer to tell you this in person," Mom said. "But I can't. Grandpa Will died last night."

I heard Rebecca wailing over the other end. Mom

said, "I've been trying to reach you all day, but evidently you've just gotten your telephone service back. Rebecca? Listen to me please." I heard Rebecca snuffling. "He had no pain and no fear. And he was old. It's sad, but it could have been much worse, and we must think of Paula now. Are you listening?"

"Yes," Rebecca mumbled.

"I want you girls to come to Paula's house tomorrow. Cecily?"

"Yes, are you all right, Mom?"

"Yes darling, I'm fine, just awfully tired. You are all all right?"

"Yes, everything here's OK. No damage or anything."

She asked to talk to Luz, and I could tell they were making arrangements about us leaving the island, and then she asked to talk to Gene, and evidently was apologizing for cutting the visit short. When the call was finished, the dinner was cold, and Rebecca didn't think we should eat at all, but we sat down anyway. All of the conversation was about leaving the next day and getting the house ready and whether Luz knew exactly how to get to Grandma Paula's and stuff like that. Even though we weren't talking about Will dying, it was all very dreary and awful, and the three males offered to clean up after dinner so we could get our act together. We let them. After all, the only thing they had to do was pack and go.

And all the time, I was also thinking, well, I guess this is the last I'll see of Clem, too. All of a sudden it was about to be all over. But there wasn't really time to dwell on it, because we were talking about who was to pack up Mom's stuff and how much, what to do about leftover food and boring things like that. We didn't really have any idea of when we'd be back, but it didn't seem as if it would be soon. We had to assume it would be a long time. We went on talking about details like that so at least we didn't have to bring up the things that were really bothering us. While I was talking about what to do with the stuff in the freezer, I was wondering if I'd ever see Clem again and what a funeral was really like. Maybe while he was talking about putting the outdoor furniture in the garage, Clem was wondering if our parents were going to get married. I figured he'd take off if that happened, so he wouldn't have to see me or either of them. But maybe he wouldn't, and then I would have to see him again, whether he wanted to or not. That's what I was thinking while I was dumping out garbage.

Also that evening people had telephone calls to make, especially Luz because she had to call a lot of my mother's friends and business associates. Luz told us that Mom said Paula was in terrible shape and Mom had to stay with her all the time. Jay was the one who had very little to do and just sat down to deal out one solitaire game after another. Each time he lost, he would mumble, "Something has gone awry." He loved that word.

The next morning was a mess, trying to load up the two cars, get everyone fed and still leave the house clean. We drove to the ferry and got the cars on, and then everyone just sat around. Jay and Rebecca talked quietly together the whole trip. That's when I felt the worst, I guess. Clem just sat there staring out at the water, and I had to fight tears over and over. Once on the dock we had hurried, horrible good-byes, and then we went our separate ways in our two cars. I felt terrible. I decided I'd better not think about anything except the immediate future, and what we had to face at Paula's.

My grandparents lived in a little house in a little town in Connecticut. It's supposed to be some kind of a joke that they live in that little house, because they used to live in a great big one, owned by my great-grandmother and run by a bunch of servants. We used to hear stories about all those people and the old days, and we used to drive by the old house every time we went to see Grandpa Will and Paula. Obviously their move had to do with money, but I never understood the family finances, and the rich time seemed such a very long ways back. I couldn't remember a time when we didn't have to be very careful about money, but it was never a hardship, it was just a fact of life. Mom earned the money, and we knew pretty much where it went. But as for anyone else in the family, I just didn't know. Grandpa Will had a rich brother somewhere, but they hadn't seen each other in years and I'd never met him. My mother had had a brother, but he had died in the Korean war. My great-grandmother had been sick in a nursing home almost ever since I was born, and evidently she had whatever family money was left. Thinking about all this on the parkway, I realized what a dope I was not to know any more than I knew about all these people. Did Mom know? All I'd heard was about how things used to be, how Paula and Will used to go to parties and on trips. I just knew them as nice old people who did bits of painting and gardening and music, and worried about Mom. She didn't like their worrying about her, I did know that.

Then I started wondering about how long we would be staying at Paula's, and how we would work it out because she only has three bedrooms. Somebody would have to sleep in Will's bed. I hoped it wasn't going to be me. The closer we got to their house, the more nervous I got. I had no idea what to expect. Would there be a lot of strangers around? How would Mom be? How did we deal with Paula? Were we supposed to cry or act brave? Rebecca was getting nervous too, because after a long silence she began to ask questions.

"Luz, what happens to the house on the island now?"

"I don't know. I think it still belongs to Great-grandma."

"Will we get to keep it?"

"I don't know."

And then she started asking about the funeral, and about how long we would have to stay, and all the stuff I'd been wondering, and we didn't have any answers for her. When we finally pulled into the driveway, it all seemed much more normal than it was, because Mom came out with a smile and told us where to put the stuff in the car. She was going to be the one to sleep in with Paula. Paula was resting just now; the doctor had given her a shot. And then it all got to be a kind of blur, because the telephone started ringing and didn't seem to stop, and people began to stop in, most of them bringing food. Mom had made the funeral arrangements, but still had things to do, and Paula stayed pretty much out of it. This went on all day and into the evening. When Paula came out, she seemed groggy and didn't want to talk at all, she just smiled tearfully at people. We kept putting food out on the dining room table, and the new people would come in and bring more. Rebecca bugged Mom for a while, how long are we staying, when can we go back to the island and all that, and Mom snapped at her and she went crying up to the room she was sharing with Luz. We didn't really sit down to dinner at all that night. We just took bits and pieces of the things people had brought. There were strangers there most of the time. One lady kept saying how different the three of us girls looked considering we were all sisters. By then Rebecca had pulled herself together and endeared herself all around by saying, "Oh it's not surprising, we have three different fathers." That shut the woman up. One old man sat around a long time, sort of drinking and crying. It was a really, really dreadful evening. I was exhausted at the end of that day, but I still had trouble going to sleep. I couldn't call on Sophia to help me out, and all night I had mixed-up dreams that seemed to just jumble through my head.

The next day was just as bad. Mom was on the telephone quite a long time with Will's brother, and the conversation upset her, although nobody dared ask her why. And there was a huge, long, emotional discussion about what we were all going to wear to the funeral, and besides all that, poor Paula still hadn't gotten her head together and had to be led through every move. Mom had to do it all.

"Mother, don't you want to take a little juice and toast, dear?"

"Oh. Why, thank you."

"Mother, it's time to get dressed now."

"Oh yes, so it is."

It was almost scary. I wondered when she was going to snap out of it. I wondered how she'd get along at the funeral, but it was as if she didn't know what was happening. In a way I felt that way too. I wasn't really taking anything in, but in a way it was nice anyway. I finally realized that Grandpa Will was really gone, and we'd just go on without him. And soon we'd find out what the changes would be.

14

Afterward, Mom said, "Rebecca, I want you and Cecily to take a long walk down by the river. It's a nice day, and it's a pretty walk, and I want the two of you to just walk or sit, away from the house, for about two hours."

We were both pleased to get out. We'd seen enough strangers and tears. It was nice of Mom to let us go. Rebecca seemed better almost as soon as we got away from the house. She said, "Remember how we used to take this walk when we were little?"

"Yes. It always seemed so far to go, but now it doesn't."

We sat down by the river bank. She said, "I wonder if we'll ever spend another summer on the island again."

"Please, Rebecca, don't start on that. We just

don't have anything to say about it, and I'm sure we'll have to wait and see."

"I guess so." She sighed. "It's so awful, being a kid. You don't have anything to say about anything."

"Well, that's not entirely true. I mean, Mom takes our feelings into consideration whenever there's a decision."

"She won't ask us how we feel about her marrying Gene."

"Do you think she's going to?"

"I think she is. Jay thinks so, too. If she does, maybe he can help us keep the house. He seems to have money enough, and he liked it there a lot."

"Well . . . that's kind of a funny way to be thinking. And I'm not sure she wouldn't ask us how we felt about it, or what she'd do if we said we didn't want her to."

"I think the decision is all made," Rebecca said. "They went through that whole thing about introducing their kids and all, and we got along fine. I mean, Luz doesn't count anyway, because she's going to have her own home soon. Jay is a horrible baboon but I think we're going to stay friends. We all got along OK. And you and Clem. I thought you had something going with Clem for a while, in fact. And then it seemed to stop? Did you? Did it fizzle or what?"

"Oh no, nothing was going," I said, and then I stopped to think. Rebecca was getting older, and she had to face things like everyone else, and besides all that, she often had a rather sensible view to offer. I decided to tell her what had happened. I said, "Well, actually that's not quite accurate."

"I knew it was a lie," she said. "So why don't you try the truth."

"OK, only it's not too easy because I'm not sure I understand it. Clem and I were really getting to be friends when he had this revelation. And it sounds nuts. But the best I can make of it, is that he thinks that if he and Gene get mixed up with our family, it would be some kind of an act of disloyalty to his mother."

"His mother!"

"See, that was my reaction exactly. That's why it's hard to explain. He still hopes his mother will come back."

"Oh, that. Yeah, a kid I know at school has that idea, too. Her father took off. He even has somebody else, and she still thinks he's going to come back. Well, if Gene marries Mom, that will cure him of that idea, won't it?"

"I guess he'll have to be cured of the idea, but I don't think it will make him feel any better about getting involved with me. He also thinks she's living in some kind of squalor while they are all so comfortable, and she's sad and lonely while they are surrounded by all the things we offer like food and flowers, and—"

"Oh bull," Rebecca said.

"Well, I'm just trying to tell you what he said."

"It's nothing like what Jay says."

"You and Jay talked about all this?"

"Well he talked about his mother a little bit. And he did say that it was much harder on Clem than on him, when she left. Even though Jay was younger. He says Clem takes everything harder than he does. It's just a difference in the way they are."

"Well what did he say about her leaving?"

"He said she was always away a lot anyhow. She didn't like it where they lived, so she used to take these huge long trips back East and romp around with all her old buddies. And she got a job; she's got something to do with jewelry design or marketing it or something like that, I'm not sure, and she never spent a lot of time hanging around her kids. And so then she just left permanently and told Gene she wanted a divorce, and got it and that was that. Jay said Clem always expected her to come back, and Jay never did. It sounds really crazy to think she might come back, because it would obviously mean coming back to Gene, not just them, and it's Gene she doesn't like."

"Yes. Gee. Did he say anything about the terrible apartment and the bad job and being lonely and all that?"

"No, he said she does a lot of things, like yoga and poetry readings, and she has friends with the same interests and all. He didn't say anything about her apartment. Although I think he sees her oftener than Clem does. I mean, I think she prefers his visits. He wouldn't bug her or get uptight the way Clem would. He doesn't tell anyone when he goes to see her, he just goes. He's very independent. He gets money from his Dad and from his grandparents, and he squirrels it away, and then when he's going to go see his grandparents, he just moseys on down to the Village and catches his mother after work. Once he went and couldn't find her, so he went to a couple of shows instead. And he's got friends in New York, too. He does a lot of stuff by himself."

"Well that's very nice, but there's still Clem. Even aside from hating to lose him as a friend, he could make things awful for all of us if Mom and Gene decide to get married. What I think is that he'd take off and never come home any more."

"No, he wouldn't, he wouldn't know where to go, he'd just mope around."

"It would still be gloomy."

"It wouldn't be any too cheery. You'd think she'd set him straight—Grace. That's Mrs. McDermott's name. I wonder why *she* doesn't cure him of his fantasy."

"Well, he said she puts a brave face on things."

"Yeah," Rebecca said. 'I bet she does. Maybe she just doesn't have the guts to say look, I split and that's it."

"After all this time?"

"However . . ." Rebecca began to get a devilish look. "It is possible she could be persuaded to spell it out for him."

"You mean . . . what do you mean?"

"I mean we could approach her directly."

"But we don't know her! We don't know anything about her."

"No, but I can easily find out. I told you, Jay's my friend. He wouldn't rat on us, not to anyone. I can get a description, and the address of the place she works and everything."

"Tell him what we're going to do?"

"Sure. It's to his best interests, too. If he has to live with all of us."

"What will you say, exactly?"

Rebecca straightened out. I hadn't seen her so enthusiastic for days. "I will explain that we are going to endeavor to extract from Grace a promise to very quickly tell Clem two things. One, that she is happy as a clam at high tide. And two, that she will never, under any circumstances, return to the home of that jerk she divorced two years ago."

"Oh my God. You can't say that."

"Well, we can take a look at her anyway. Get an idea."

"Talk about getting into other people's business."

"Well that's not it, really. If they're going to be

our brothers, we might have to meet her sometime anyway. I mean, she's important to us, whether she wants to be or not."

"Would you tell her that her ex-husband might be marrying our mother?"

"I don't know. We'll just have to see when we get there. We'll do it as soon as we can after we get home."

"Yeah."

"There's no time to lose," Rebecca said. She jumped up and brushed the grass off her skirt. "Let's walk until our two hours are up," she said.

15

When we got back to Paula's, Mom told us we were all going home the next day, and she added very firmly that we were not going to discuss anything until we got there. And that included the three or more hours on the parkway. This put rather a damper on conversation, but then we were all tired anyway, so we didn't mind too much. We left rather late the next day—she did let us sleep as long as we wanted to. Some friend of Paula's was moving in for a few days when we left. We also left a bit of a mess since we'd had a sort of brunch around one; but the friend said never mind, she would take care of it.

So one more time we packed all our junk in the car, and this time we headed home. We were even more tired when we got there, and Mom announced that she was taking us all out to dinner at a little cheap neighborhood restaurant we go to sometimes. It's the kind of place where there's a bar in the front, and guys sit around watching television, but you can get a pretty good Italian dinner in the back, where we went. The people there know us, so they asked Mom how business was, and she said fine. They seem to think she's a lawyer, because they saw her play one once on a show, and they couldn't quite believe that wasn't what she did for a living. Once the greetings were over, we settled down and ordered, and when Mom had her glass of wine, she started her chat.

"We're going to have to make some changes," she said. "First of all, I want you to understand what happened to my mother. It wasn't just that she was grieved at the loss of Grandpa Will, although that is certainly a bad enough blow for her. But there's more to it. The way my grandmother's will is written, the money does not go from her sons to their wives on her death, so Paula will not have the money she expected to have in her old age. Will would have left his share to her, of course, if he had outlived his mother, as he expected to do. But he didn't, so he had nothing to leave. She has no money and cannot expect to get any later on."

I was still trying to digest this when Rebecca piped up, ahead of me as usual. "Who gets Will's share when Great-grandma dies?"

"I do," Mom said.

We were all pretty surprised, except for Luz, who

just sat there looking pretty and drinking her wine. I was sure Mom had already explained all this to her and was a little annoyed I hadn't been included the first time around. I tried to swallow my jealousy and understand what this meant.

"I will get Will's share when my Grandma Kellogg dies, but in the meantime and for the rest of her life, I will be financially responsible for Paula. And I must tell you that Will's share of the estate will not represent half of it, because he borrowed against it during his life. He made almost no money, nor did Paula, and he used up his income and borrowed against his share of the estate. So I will not be rich when she dies, I will only be better able to take care of all of us and my mother."

This time we sat for quite a while. Then Rebecca was the first to speak again. "What does this mean about the house on the island?"

"The house on the island still belongs to my grandmother. Her attorneys have been paying the taxes for her; but I spoke to my uncle, who will inherit half of it when she dies, and he will not want it, of course. We would have to buy out his share and maintain it ourselves, which I cannot afford to do. It wouldn't be a wise investment of the money I will inherit, whenever that happens. And in fact he wants to sell it now. He'd been trying to persuade Will to sell it for years—if both were agreed, they could have approached her representatives on it."

It sounded complicated and boring. I thought I really should try to understand, though, and at least not let the house get sold without understanding why. I said, "Can he sell it without your permission?"

"No, but if it's not sold, the estate continues to support it, and that money comes out of my share. It's a bad way to have money tied up."

Luz spoke up now, rather breathlessly. "I told Mom that maybe I might buy it. There are a couple of things that might happen to bring me some money, and Parkes already has money, and he might like to buy it."

Mom was smiling nicely, and so was I; but I didn't believe there was any hope, and I didn't think she did either. Rebecca said, "But if it's a bad investment for Mom, it's a bad investment for you or Parkes."

"Not really, because Mom needs her money in a place where it produces income, but I can put mine somewhere where it might go up in value in years to come, because I may not have to have so much income."

Rebecca continued to stare at her, maybe surprised she knew a little about something Rebecca didn't know anything about. Then Luz said, "Neither of you has said anything about the fact that Paula will have to come live with us."

This was a real shocker. As far as I was concerned— and I'm sure Rebecca felt the same way—it was really bad news. Rebecca said, "But why?"

"Well, obviously it's because I can't afford to pay

for two households. She owns the house, but there are still taxes and utilities and upkeep."

It wasn't that I didn't like Paula. It was just that she would hate living with us, hate losing her own home. No wonder she had been acting like such a nut—she had to move in with us and must have known it. Everyone else must have been thinking along the same lines, about stretching and sharing our space.

Rebecca said, "If Great-grandma Kellogg dies pretty soon, you could let her stay in her own house, couldn't you? I mean, then you could afford it?"

"Yes, then I could. But the lady is alive and could live for years, so there's no point in thinking along those lines. My father did, and it was disastrous." There was a little bitterness in her tone, I thought. I suspected she had feelings she wasn't letting on about. More and more I realized that there were whole places in the adult world I'd never even looked into, about money, and the past, and how people felt.

Mom said, "Of course all this won't happen immediately. She will have to sell her house, and that usually takes a couple of months."

I said, "Wouldn't Will's brother be able to help take care of Paula?"

"He has declined to help," Mom said. She said it very flatly.

"Well where are we going to put her?" Rebecca asked. "Under the dining table?"

"She will take the other bed in my room."

Mom's closet was floor-to-ceiling belongings. So were all her drawers. She was very organized, so that she could grab the right shoes and scarf and handbag and sweater or whatever and get dressed in two minutes, but there was no extra space.

Luz said, "I'll be able to leave very soon, and she can put some of her things in our room, Rebecca."

"What will Grandma do with all her furniture and stuff like that? She has about six tons of sheet music, and the old piano, and about three hundred scrap books, and—"

"We don't have to solve every single detail right this moment," Mom said, and it suddenly occurred to me that she was about to break down right then. She was trying to hide how upset she was.

I said quickly, "Listen, we're all terribly clever women; we are going to work this out just fine. Let's just take a while to get used to it and not think about it any more just now. We'll get it all beautifully solved when the time comes. Luz and Mom have to go back to work in just a couple of days, so I suggest they rest and take it easy until then."

"Thank you," Mom said. "There's one more thing we're all going to do, though. Before I turn the car in."

"What's that?"

"We're going to drive up to the country tomorrow and visit Great-grandma Kellogg in the nursing home."

One more shocker. I wanted to ask Mom more questions, like about the island house and if we could go back before it was sold, but I didn't think this was the time. She'd let us know sooner or later. I looked at Rebecca in hopes of sending her a message about keeping her mouth shut, but her mouth was already shut. I guess she was in mild shock from all the bad news, like Luz and me. Luz already knew everything. I decided to put away my jealousy about that. It didn't help anything.

16

It was horribly hot and muggy the next day. A perfect day to be on the island. But we were on the parkway again instead. None of us wanted to go. But when Mom is determined, you don't win by fighting her. In fact you don't win any way. Very little was said in the car on the way up. It seemed to me that there was a lot that wasn't solved, but it would all have to wait. I wondered when she was going to see Gene again, but I didn't even dare ask. Mom volunteered that places like the one our great-grandmother was in could be rather sad, and she also said that Great-grandma wouldn't know who we were since she hadn't recognized anyone in years. I wondered why we were going. I guess she just thought we ought to see our great-grandmother once before she died. If she ever died.

We were all still tired, and we were also hot and probably nervous and upset. When we pulled into the nursing home, all I could think was that at least it was probably cool inside. The place looked like a gigantic motel, all on one level. Inside it looked a little like that too, everything all bright and cheerful. Except the people. You saw them right away, sitting around in wheel chairs with cheery nurses pushing them around. I didn't want to look too closely at anything. When we got to the main desk, Mom told the nurse who we were, and we went to the room. There were two people in the two beds, and one of them was yelling at the nurse.

"Please, dear, just take a swallow," the nurse was saying. That lady wasn't our relative. The other lady was. She was tiny. She looked like an old, old doll, with white hair and bright blue eyes.

In her best modulated stage voice, Mom said, "Hello, Grandma. It's Kristin. I've brought my three daughters to see you."

The eyes seemed to be trying to find us, and she seemed to be trying to speak. The nurse said, "Isn't this nice, Mrs. Kellogg? Aren't you happy to see your visitors?" She turned to Mom. "She's so good, your grandma. She never gives us any trouble at all. Uh . . . you look just like you do on TV, Miss Kellogg."

"I suppose I do," Mom said graciously.

"Oh yes. You're one of my favorites." The nurse giggled a little nervously.

"Why thank you!"

The nurse didn't want to go. She thought she was getting to see a celebrity. Then she stared at Luz, and you could tell she knew she'd seen her in some magazine. Mom said, "Don't feel you have to stay, I'm sure you have other things to do."

"I'll just let you have your little visit with Grandma, then," the nurse said, taking the hint and leaving.

Mom took her grandmother's hand. She said, "Grandma, you look very pretty. My daughters are all very pretty too, aren't they?"

She did seem to be trying to look at us. "Take her hand," Mom said to me.

"Hello, Great-grandmother," I said, feeling like a jerk. I took her little hand. It was cool. Mom made the others do the same. The old lady seemed several times to be trying to speak, but then she gave up. After a little while she seemed to doze off.

We sat there not knowing whether it was more polite to look at her or look away. But even the way she was, I realized for the first time that she was a real person. And I also understood then that that was exactly why Mom had brought us here—to show us she was a real person. She must have been pretty. I tried to remember things I'd heard about her . . . she had marvelous parties, and played the violin, and sometimes said outrageous things. And I thought, she certainly never had any idea she was going to wind up like this, or be a problem for anyone. It was probably the last thing she would have wanted, having everyone else have control over her life and being powerless. She woke up again and seemed to be aware that there were people there because she became a little agitated.

"We don't want to tire her," Mom said. Very quietly, as if we were sneaking, we all crept out. We went back down the corridor and then out to the car.

All of a sudden I thought of Clem. I wondered why I would be thinking of him at a time like that. Then I decided it was because I didn't really understand this visit, there was something I hadn't taken in. Maybe by talking about it I would understand. And maybe not. Maybe you only put everything together after you've seen and done other things, and then a pattern emerges.

I didn't know what I'd learned, exactly, but I did feel as if I'd had a new experience. We got in the car and pulled out. Nobody said anything for a long time.

Finally Rebecca piped up. She said, "Could we stop somewhere for hamburgers before we go home?"

17

"Please," Sophia said, "Please keep me as the only hostage, and let all the other passengers go."

"I cannot do that," the dark young man said, his machine gun at the ready. His English was good, though heavily accented. "But you are very brave."

"I am not brave," Sophia said, tossing her head. "I merely have a respect for other human beings, which evidently you have not."

"The respect must be for our political prisoners. But we have discussed this many times these past three days. You will not change my views."

"No, I hoped only to soften your heart."

"That, I think you have done."

"Then will you let the others go?"

"Perhaps. Then it will be easier to keep you. . . ."

"Ceecee."

"Go away, Rebecca."

"Cecily!"

"Go away, Rebecca. I'm sleeping."

"You are not. You have to get up. I have your grapefruit juice here for you. And if you don't get up, I'm going to pour it all over your head."

"Oh, go away." I got up. "What's the matter with you? We don't have anything special to do today."

"Oh yes we do. Mom and Luz have gone back to work, and Mom is having a drink with Gene tonight before she comes home. So there's no time to lose in our project."

"I'm scared. I don't want to do it."

"You can't chicken out now. They might get engaged this very day."

I drank my grapefruit juice, and when I'd stopped wincing, I said, "This may be a very bad idea."

"Grace McDermott is going to have a little surprise today," Rebecca said, ignoring my value judgment.

I said, "Why are you so keen on going to see her?"

"Number one, because if Gene and Mom get married, it will be bad enough without having Clem mess it up; and if his mother can set him straight, it will help a lot. And number two, it would be nice if you and Clem got back together."

I looked at her suspiciously. "And number three, four and five, if nobody stops Mom and Gene from getting married, she can afford to keep the house on the island."

"I never even thought of that," Rebecca said. She's a first-rate liar so I wasn't sure. I just sighed and started to get dressed. She stood there smiling.

"You're a wicked little rat," I said.

We took a bus downtown. It was hot again, and the town was full of tourists. All those millions of people who say New York is a nice place to visit but they wouldn't want to live there must have been visiting. It took me the whole trip to wake up. We got off at Washington Square, and I said, "Listen, before we strike out, maybe we ought to sit down by the fountain and decide on our strategy."

"Yeah, OK, I have a plan."

We sat down. "I hope you have all the information we need."

"I have it committed to memory." She gave me the name and address of the shop.

"What does she look like? Boys are usually awful at giving descriptions."

"Jay's not. Get this. She's medium tall, thin, has shoulder-length brown hair and brown eyes. She has a long thin nose and a wide mouth and she doesn't wear much makeup, but she wears half a ton of jewelry."

"That sounds like about half the women in New York. So OK, what are you going to say to her?"

"We're going to ask her to lunch because we're friends of her sons."

"And what if she refuses?"

"Then we tell her we have to talk to her anyway because it's important."

"Yeah. Oh dear."

"Come on Cecily, don't be such a pussycat. Let's go find the shop."

It was only a few blocks away, and we didn't have any trouble finding it. Once inside, contrary to my expectation, we spotted her immediately, and she was a lot more attractive than the description. She looked rather serious, and she had on sandals and a long cotton skirt and T-shirt and didn't especially look like anybody's mother, although I'm not sure how that looks. She saw us and said with a polite smile, "May I help you?"

I wanted to give up right then. She was a real person, Clem's mother, and I felt terrible. I looked at the jewelry.

Rebecca said, "Ms McDermott?"

A little surprised, she said, "Yes . . . ?"

"I'm Rebecca Kellogg and this is my sister Cecily. We'd like to talk to you. May we take you to lunch?"

I looked at her, and she looked rather blank. "What was it you wanted to talk about?"

"We're friends of your sons, and it's personal."

Grace did not look at all pleased. She said, "Did

someone ask you to come here, or was it your idea?"

"It was our idea. But it's important."

She looked uncertain. It occurred to me that she might not even believe we knew her sons. Odd things do happen, especially in big cities. I said, "Clem and Jay spent part of their vacation with us at our summer house. And now we'd like very much to discuss with you something that, uh, came up during that time."

Mentioning the names did help. She said, "We won't have lunch. If you like, you can come back at twelve-thirty, and we'll go up to my apartment."

It was agreed, and we left. Rebecca was jubilant. She said, "Grace probably thinks one or both of us is pregnant."

We wandered around the streets, muddling our way through the masses. I said, "She didn't look terribly friendly."

"Well, after all, she ran away from them, so she can't be the type that really treasures the opportunity to get to know all their little friends. And she has to think it's trouble."

"Well, in a way she's right."

"Listen, Ceecee, she's a really cool cookie. This may not be as easy as we thought."

"I never for one minute thought it would be easy. And you can do the talking because I wouldn't even know where to start."

There are shops in the village that Rebecca and I

like, so we didn't have any trouble filling the time until twelve-thirty. We showed up promptly. Grace looked even less pleased than she had before, now that she'd had time to think it over. We walked to her apartment, which was not very far. She let us in the door, and my first thought was, Clem doesn't know anything about New York apartments if he thinks this is deprivation. It was small, but it was very nice. The stuff in it wasn't wildly expensive but very attractive. Maybe Clem thought it was bad because it was on a sort of a dirty street, but then what street isn't. I also felt that we didn't belong there at all.

Grace McDermott sat down, and so did we. She said, "What is the problem." Flat, not like a question.

Rebecca said, "Gene might be marrying our mother, and Clem might be making trouble."

I couldn't believe it. Rebecca had a way of plunging right into the heart of the matter, but this was too much.

Ms McDermott said, "You can't believe that that has anything at all to do with me."

"Yes it has, because Clem and Ceecee, I mean Cecily, were getting to be friends, but Clem thought it would be disloyal to you if they kept it up, so they stopped because of his crazy ideas. And Clem thinks you might go back to them, and nobody in their family should get mixed up with anyone in our family because you might be going back."

My heart was sinking. It didn't even make sense to

me, how could it make sense to this chilly lady sitting there on her white sofa, looking so displeased. She got up and got a cigarette and lit it, and sat back down. She was probably figuring out what to answer to this mess. She turned to me and said, "I don't believe I quite understand. Since you're the one with the relationship with Clem, perhaps you could explain to me why it is you're here."

Oh misery. How could I tell her Clem thought her life was a mess, when she looked so self-contained in her nice tidy apartment full of plants and books and pictures. I also suddenly realized that as Rebecca had said, a woman who had left her kids couldn't be expected to suddenly develop an interest. I wish I'd taken that more seriously.

"It's just more or less the way Rebecca explained it," I said. "And I do think Clem has a misunderstanding about your situation."

"What situation? This all sounds like adolescent drama to me. It makes very little sense, and I don't think I care to get involved."

I was beginning not to like this woman. All you have to do is say something like "adolescent drama" and inwardly I go into a raving snit. I said, "We didn't come here to get you involved. We only thought you could explain your situation to Clem, so that he wouldn't feel so guilty about whatever happens."

"Look," she said, stubbing out her cigarette and

looking as if she wished it was us. "I don't know whether you want your mother to marry Gene, or whether you want the way paved for some sort of a relationship between you and Clem. Or both. Whatever your motives, it's clear that you came here in your own self-interest. You want me to somehow magically fix things up to suit your own wishes."

"That's not true," I said, really teed off now. "It's much more to Clem's interest than mine."

"You seem to believe that by saying certain words that you have all prepared for me, everything will fall into place just the way you want it."

"No," I said.

Rebecca said, "Ms McDermott, please don't think we're here because we're so keen on our mother marrying Gene. Our mother—"

"I am not at all interested in your mother," Grace said. It was the wrong name for her, I thought. "That is none of my business, and I don't intend to have you or anyone else try to make it my business."

"But she may become the stepmother of your sons!"

"I have no control over who becomes the stepmother of my sons."

Rebecca looked nonplussed, but she forged onward anyhow. "The thing is, see, can't you understand we're not talking about what's your business or your control, we're talking about Clem. He's all mixed up with his father and our mother and you."

"What you're saying is simply that Clem is all mixed up. Why do you believe that a few words from me will suddenly change his whole attitude? The truth is that he cannot adjust to facts, he refuses to accept facts. Piling them up or repeating them does not improve his chances of accepting them."

Rebecca said, "You could at least tell him there's no way you're going back and that you're perfectly happy. You could at least try."

"Oh what utter nonsense! You seem a very clever and aggressive little girl, but you are nevertheless a child. You understand nothing, and yet you have the audacity to come here and tell me how I feel about my life and what to say to my sons. I suggest that instead of attempting to teach me something about which I know more than you do, you try learning something: stay out of other people's business. Just handling your own is a big enough job."

Rebecca was angry to the soul. She looked as if she were about to pick up the big glass ash tray and heave it. She said, "It would really be a pleasure to stay out of your business if we could. The trouble is you adults have such a hard time getting your business straightened out that the mess pours all over us."

Now it was McDermott who was going to heave something. Her eyes were flashing fire. She said, "Don't make a judgment on how well my life is or is not straightened out. If you are going to make such judgments about adults, at least pick on the ones you know. And now I think we have nothing more to say to each other so I suggest you go back to wherever you came from."

We stomped out in a deafening silence, and she closed the door behind us. We stomped for several blocks before we stopped to pull ourselves together. Finally Rebecca turned to me with her eyes shooting out flaming sparks and said, "What an incredible bitch."

"I wasn't drawn to her myself," I said, a little shakily. "I can't even say I've been thrown out of better places. Maybe she has to be nasty because she's suffering from guilt about leaving her kids."

"I don't think she's suffering from anything except bitchiness. I take that back, she's not suffering at all, it's everyone else. Clem should be tickled to death that he doesn't have to live with that monster. Every day he should get up and say a prayer of gratitude that his mother left home."

"Now he'll never speak to any of us," I said sadly. "Not that he was going to. Mummy will tell him that these two horrid little adolescent girls came and told her how to run her life and please tell his friends to mind their own business. And he'll be furious that we interfered."

"I suppose so. Jay didn't care. He seemed to think it was sort of funny that we were going to approach her."

"Hilarious," I said weakly. "We really should have known, though. You made the point yourself. She did leave. We couldn't expect her to be all full of interest and sympathy."

"I just wanted her to tell Clem she wasn't coming back. He should be so lucky. Did you notice that I went from adolescent to child in absolutely no time?"

All the way home on the bus, we talked about her. We talked about the apartment and how Clem didn't understand, and about how she looked, and how she dealt with the boys. We went over everything that was said, and speculated about Gene and why she left him. And we wondered who all she would tell about the visit and how soon, and what she would say about us. By the time we got home we were a bit nervous about when and what would come out of our little visit. We decided to clean the apartment and make a nice dinner, which we spent the rest of the afternoon doing.

18

Luz came home first, tired because she'd been up since very early on some job. We hadn't discussed what we would tell her. Rebecca raised her eyebrows in a questioning way at me, and I nodded. That was very delicate of Rebecca considering her nature, but then again she can be sneaky as well as forthright. She said, "Luz, we want to talk to you about something."

"Could it wait until after my bath? I want to be out of the bathroom by the time Mom gets home."

"No. Because we want to tell you before she comes. I don't know when she'll hear it, and she may not hear about it at all, and if she doesn't you don't have to tell her, but—"

"Oh no, Rebecca, please don't tell me something I'm supposed to keep from Mom."

Rebecca stopped short for a change. I don't think she knew how not to go on. I said, "OK, we won't. It isn't anything awful, Luz, don't worry."

"Whatever it is, I wish you'd tell her. She's very good about . . . when . . . she's OK to tell things to. I'm going for my bath."

She vanished. Rebecca and I exchanged glances and shrugged. I wondered if Rebecca was having the same thought I was, that Luz had obviously taken some sort of problem to Mom, and Mom had helped. Not that this was a surprise. I was beginning to wonder if maybe we hadn't better tell Mom. That way it wouldn't be news if she heard it from someone else. I decided that after dinner I would approach Rebecca on this privately. It might give us an advantage, actually.

Luz came out of the tub, got into a kaftan and came into the living room and started reading *Women's Wear Daily*. Rebecca was reading *The Village Voice*, and I was reading *New York Magazine*. We heard Mom's key in the lock, and then her steps in the little hall; and even before she came in, we knew all was not well. When she appeared in the doorway, there was no question about it—she was breathing fire.

"We had better have a discussion right now," she said, in her low, controlled, well-modulated, dangerous voice. She crossed the room and sat down gracefully and then turned to Rebecca and me. "I'd like to know exactly what it is you two thought you were doing when you paid a call on Grace McDermott today, and exactly what was said."

Well that was a clear enough question. Now all we had to do was answer. Luckily for me, Rebecca never knew when she wasn't supposed to be in charge. She instantly wailed, "Oh, Mummy, it was for Clem and Ceecee. They were just getting to really relate to each other, and then Clem turned it all off because he felt guilty about his Mom, and so . . . how did you hear so fast?"

"Grace called Gene at work, which she hasn't done for years. And I was seeing him after work anyway. Does that answer your question?"

"Yes."

"All right. Go on."

"Well, that was really about it," Rebecca said. "I mean, it was because of Clem mostly."

"I believe that was *not* about it," Mom said. "Unless she was simply making this all up for obscure reasons, you demanded that she take an interest because I was going to become her son's stepmother!"

"Might. Might. I only said you might. I never said you would."

For a moment there was silence. Luz was sitting there invisible in her chair in the corner, looking big-eyed at all of us. Mom turned to me. "Was it said that I might become stepmother to the boys?"

I croaked out, "Well, you see, Clem—"

"If you please, I should like to wait for a moment

before we get to Clem. I would like to clear up what it was you said to a total stranger about *me!* Why did you not tell *me* what you had in mind? Why did you go rushing off to force your speculations on a total stranger? Why did you take it upon yourselves to simply approach an unsympathetic and cold person with something you could easily have brought to me?"

Rebecca started to cry. Mom was not deterred. She said, "It's very clear that you knew you were doing the wrong thing or you would not have gone behind my back. I never expected an act of disloyalty from either one of you, and I'm very, very disappointed."

Crying would have been as good a move as any, but I felt too sick to cry. Recent events had been bad enough, and now I'd totally messed up by hurting Mom, which I never meant to do. I hadn't thought about her part in it, which was just as bad. I'd been unthinking and stupid. I just sat staring down at the carpet and feeling hopeless.

"Before I speak to each of you individually about this, there is one other point I want to cover."

I looked up. What other point could there possibly be? She said, "Is there any chance that either or both of you were promoting a marriage between Gene and me in order to save the house?"

We both instantly said no. She studied our faces. Then she turned to Luz. "Did you know anything about this plan?"

Luz just shook her head, startled. Rebecca said, almost disdainfully, "Of course she didn't."

Mom signaled Rebecca to follow her into her room, while Luz and I just sat there. I knew Luz wouldn't say anything, and she didn't; but somehow I felt I ought to make some comment. I said, "It was a rotten thing to do, I guess, although I wasn't thinking of it in terms of Mom at all. It was just selfish not to—I just wanted to fix it so that Clem could be friends with me again; he said he couldn't because his mother might come back. It's all so complicated. I feel awful."

"Well it's been an unusual summer for all of us I guess," Luz said. "I'm sure Mom will realize it was only just not thinking, not trying to be mean."

We waited and waited for Rebecca. It was like waiting for a verdict, except we already had the verdict. Guilty. Me too. Then Rebecca went to her own room, and I was called in to where Mom holds court. It's a pretty room, all yellow and white flowers. It's cheerful and ladylike, like Mom. But it's like Mom inside, too—all business. Ask her where the lavender cardigan is, and she'll say, "In the left top drawer underneath the yellow one." I sat down on the little ruffled inquisition chair. Of course she seemed perfectly calm. She said, "I'd like to hear what you have to say." What a lousy beginning.

"It's my fault. I should have known better. I wanted to get Clem back. I'm really sorry. I wasn't thinking about you when I should have been. I was thinking about Clem and me."

"Neither you nor Rebecca blames the other, and I'm glad of that."

"I'm older, though."

"Yes. I wouldn't ordinarily ask about your relationship with Clem because I would consider it personal, but now that you've taken it out of the realm of the personal and involved others, you'd better tell me about it."

So now I started to cry. Unlike Rebecca, I didn't mean to or want to, it just happened. It was painful. Mom just slid the Kleenex box toward me and waited. How many times has she done that in her life, I wondered. I said, "Ever since the end of the first week they were there, I've been miserable about *something*. Sometimes two or three things." I snuffled on, and finally began to tell her the whole thing: how I was scared of boys and felt really backward in experience, and how I started getting to know him in such a weird way that I wasn't scared, and how we got along so well that I just fell in love with him. And how terrible it was when he started in with Alissa, and then the conversation we had after the hurricane, which made me think that somehow we ought to be able to work something out. And telling Rebecca, and how we decided we could make it work out.

When I finally ran down, she said, "So it hinged a great deal on whether or not Gene and I married. Did you seriously think I would marry him?"

"I don't know; everyone else seemed to think so. I can't always tell how you feel about things and people.

I thought you'd like to be married, but I didn't know how desperate you were—oh, I don't mean that, he's not bad, you're not desperate—"

She finally laughed a little bit, which helped, so I laughed a little bit and blew my nose again. She said, "I am not desperate at all, as a matter of fact. My life is in most ways quite good just as it is. I thought you realized that. I have you girls and my work and my friends. Gene is simply one of them. I couldn't marry him. He is an entirely decent person, but he has rather rigid views, which would make me uncomfortable in a marriage. So that settles that, and I wish you'd asked me. As to Clem . . . I suspect that having his mother leave the family gave him a fear of having a close relationship with a female, for fear the next one would abandon him, too."

That was one of her Psychological Explanations. She's big on those and I usually mistrust them. However, I began to realize, I didn't find them quite so hard to accept if they were applied to someone other than myself. I said, "If that's true it's a pretty tough case to solve. How can I?"

"I don't think you can. If you represent a threat to him, you're not going to get anywhere. If he wants to try trusting you, he will; and if he doesn't dare, any kind of pressure will just send him further away."

"He's pretty far away right now. He might as well be in the USSR for all the pressure I can put on him. And—well, if there was any hope of his coming back when he finds out you and Gene aren't going to get married, I guess I blew it today. He'll hear about it and never forgive me."

"Maybe. You'll have to wait and see. He did seem to talk quite frankly with you, which is a major form of trust. He didn't have to, after all. But I do think you'll just have to wait for him and not pursue the matter yourself, not that it's your style to pursue."

"It's certainly not. I spend most of my time running. So I guess that's that."

"I'm sorry about all this. But . . . maybe if he really has himself talked into this theory about his mother's discomfort, once he finds out Gene and I are not going to marry, he'll come cautiously back to see if you're as nice as he thought you were."

"Unless he's horrified that I talked to his mother."

"Well, I suppose it's remotely possible he could take that as a caring gesture. By the way, I wonder why you thought you could influence his mother in any positive way? It would be her natural reaction to be hostile, because as far as she's concerned anything wrong in her children's minds must not be taken as being due to her behavior. She has to feel that way in order to survive, I would guess."

"Yes. It was dumb."

"Well, we're an hour late for dinner, and I have to see someone in half an hour so we'd better eat now."

19

It hardly seemed possible, but there was half the summer left. There was also a big fat problem with Paula, which was that for the moment she really was hardly able to take care of herself, and the neighbors couldn't do it anymore. She was quite unable to get her house ready for sale. So Rebecca and I were elected to do it. A real estate lady told us what to do, and we did it. The house was perfectly clean and kept up, because what Paula and Grandpa Will had mostly done, was just keep their house up. About all Paula could do to help us was arrange flowers and clear the table, so we kept asking her to do those things. We got rid of all Will's clothes when she wasn't looking, and we threw out a lot of stuff, mostly old magazines and bottles and things like that. We did the marketing and cooking and cleaning up, and we showed the house to the people who came to see it. When we did that, Grandma Paula sat out on her little porch, smiling and letting the tears run down her cheeks. We didn't blame her, since she had lost her husband and was just about to lose her home and belongings and independence, but it was still awful. Rebecca and I kept looking at each other when that happened. Trying to be helpful, Rebecca once said, "Grandma Paula, Great-grandma Kellogg is sure to die soon, and then you can come back."

"No," Paula said sweetly. "She'll live to be well over a hundred. And by then I'll be into my eighties."

There wasn't much we could say to that. However, it was a relief when she said things that made sense, because she didn't always.

Mom decided that when we'd finished with Paula's little house, and had everything ready so that the rest of the stuff could just be packed up and put into storage, we should take Paula to the island. And we should get that house ready to sell too, although it wouldn't be likely to sell as fast. We were going to sell it furnished, so all we had to do was put tags on the things we were going to take out of the house. We were supposed to find out which things Paula wanted to keep, and that turned out to be a much harder job than I had any idea it would be. Like, I took her into the playroom, which we had completely cleaned, and said, "Grandma, what do you want taken out of here?"

"Oh, I don't know, dear. Don't you think we should

leave it just as it is? Everything here was bought for the room, nothing was make-do."

"OK," I said, although I had a feeling she had momentarily forgotten we were going to sell the house.

And then she seemed to remember. She said plaintively, "I did always especially like that little Indian rug. I bought it in nineteen hundred and sixty-five because Will's old dog ate the other one. Wasn't that an odd thing for him to do! Although one of the dogs we had when the children were young was much odder. She ate an entire string of Christmas tree light bulbs."

"Oh my. Well then I'll tag the Indian rug." I wondered what we were going to do with the things she wanted to keep. And hard as this must be for her, it was hard for me, too. There was a terrible ache in my throat all the time. Rebecca was almost in tears quite a bit, too.

"On the other hand, it's not terribly valuable, really. And it may be worn, too, being where it is."

"Shall I leave it then?"

"Well, let's see how much else there is."

We moved on to the living room. "OK, what things do you want to keep from this room?"

"Well, the good clock will definitely go to your mother's. Grandma Kellogg bought it in Germany in the early thirties, and nobody really understood why she brought it here, where things rust so badly."

I took out one of the tags marked "Does Not Go With House" and put it on. Then she said, "But on the other hand it hasn't worked in years. Perhaps it would cost more to fix it than it's worth." Tag off.

So it went. "I've always loved this Wedgewood, it's one of my favorite china patterns. It would be lovely to have it in my own little place some time." Tag on. "But then again, almost all of it is quite chipped, and I do have all that Spode." Tag off. I had a feeling the entire exercise was in vain, and I was also very sorry for her. I was a little bit sorry for me, too, may as well admit it, and I still thought about Clem about ninety percent of the time, wondering what he was doing, what he was thinking. I was torn between pity and irritation, self-pity and boredom, longing and grieving, and a big batch of other emotions. I spent a lot of time on the beach just walking.

I only talked to people, other than Rebecca, if I had to. We didn't go out nights; we didn't feel like it, either one of us, and we didn't feel really comfortable about leaving Paula alone at night. We knew she was nervous and didn't sleep until we were upstairs. In fact, if we wanted to do anything when she wanted to go to bed, we just went upstairs and did it because she felt better when we were there. Dave hung around quite a bit. Nobody minded that. Mom came up for a couple of weekends, and in two hours she had tagged everything she wanted from the house. Luz couldn't come again at all. She had too many jobs. But that was really good news in a way. She wanted so badly to feel successful. I felt a lot better about her than I had at the beginning of the summer.

Paula seemed to get a better grip on herself. We decided that she really could go back to her house until it was sold and take care of herself all right. She wasn't terrific, but she seemed a little better for the moment.

Then, suddenly the summer was over. It was time to go home and get ready for school. I'd be a senior but I felt a lot older than that. I went to bed in my blue and green room that night and cried myself to sleep. So much was gone, so much was different, so much was worse.

20

Luz was away making a commercial the second night Rebecca and I were back from the island. So there were only two of us for Mom to gather for her latest piece of news. I figured it couldn't possibly be good, and braced myself.

Mom said, "When Auden and I separated, I told him that if he ever gave up drinking I would go back. Some time ago he joined Alcoholics Anonymous, and he's not had a drink for an entire year. And so . . ." She smiled a little. But Rebecca let out a howl like an animal.

"Daddy's coming back," she said, almost in a whisper now. "Daddy's coming back!" She ran to Mom and let herself be hugged.

I was thrilled, too. After all, he was the only father

I'd ever known. I was grinning like an idiot. Rebecca was crying and laughing and alternately jumping up and down and hugging Mom. Finally she said, "When?"

"It's not set yet. I saw a lot of him this summer. I didn't want to say anything until I was absolutely certain it was going to be all right, but now I am."

"I never guessed it!" Rebecca said. "I can't understand why I never guessed it, all those Sundays last year. It never crossed my mind that this was kind of . . . testing, or that he might ever come back."

"It wasn't meant to," Mom said, just a little smugly.

"Now we'll definitely have to put Paula under the dining table," Rebecca said.

"I was thinking of putting you there," Mom said. She looked happy.

"Well really, when Luz goes, it won't be bad because Ceecee and I will share a room and Paula can take Ceecee's."

"Cecily," I said. "Please."

"Does Daddy have a good job now? If he has, maybe we can get a bigger apartment."

"Well, maybe, and we've even talked about moving to the country. The commute will mean much less to me now that you two are older."

"Oh Daddy's coming home! When do I get to see him?"

"Any minute. He's due here in just a little while."

It was then that the telephone rang. I got it, so Rebecca could carry on about Dad all she wanted with Mom.

"Cecily?"

"Yeah." My heart skipped several beats.

"This is Clem."

"Yeah, hi Clem."

"Hi. How've you been?"

"Not too bad. You?"

"OK. You sound breathless."

"Do I? Well I guess that's because Mom said our Dad is coming back."

"I heard they'd been seeing each other this summer. So. Is that good news?"

"I think so."

"I guess you can't talk right now. Anyhow, I have something funny to tell you. My Dad has this new chick, and she has two *little boys*. Can you believe it?"

"That is pretty funny. Especially after the way it could have been."

"That's what I mean."

"So when do you start college, Clem?"

"Next week. So anyway, I have to come to town tomorrow, and I thought we could do something if you're not too busy."

"Sure, no problem." So in a daze, I made a date with Clem. I was actually going to see him the next day. There was a lot to talk about. I hung up. Changes all around. A new chance for Clem and me, and for Auden and my Mom, even for Rebecca and Luz. With Auden around, things would probably be better even for Paula. Well. We could all use it.

The gypsy violins were playing softly. "I wish we could sit here forever," the dark-eyed young man was saying. "Please, Sophia, tell me you love me."

Sophia sighed. "I cannot tell you that, Omar. There is someone else."

"You break my heart."

"I am truly sorry."

"Let me see your hand," he said. "I have a special gift . . . ah, I see you have a happy family. I see a young man who loves you." He looked at her sadly. "Yes, he is the one. It will be a long friendship. And I see a house, a house on the island."

"It was the house of my childhood summers," Sophia said with a rueful smile. "It is mine no more."

"Ah, but this is a different house, a smaller one, soon to be purchased by someone else, perhaps by more than one person."

"Would that such a thing could happen!"

Suddenly someone approached them, someone with brown hair and blue jeans. He was very familiar.

"That's not Sophia, you jerk," Clem said. "That's Cecily. So why don't you buzz off, you stupid looking jackass."

"This must be the rude American boy who has this lady's heart," Omar said.

"That's right. So disappear."

Omar disappeared. Cecily stood up, leaving Sophia fading behind her. Cecily said, "I may not be needing you for a while, Sophia. It's just possible that this ordinary boy is the one I'm going to be dealing with for a while. And I may even be able to manage him alone."

"Of course you will, my dear," Sophia said. "Good luck." And she disappeared, too.

Cecily took Clem's hand, and they stepped outside onto the beach. There they walked hand in hand into the sunset.